WHOEVER HAD JUST RETURNED THESE BOOKS HAD NEVER INTENDED TO DO IT IN DAYLIGHT. . . .

Kathleen turned her attention to the volume on torture. She started to turn the front cover, but the book fell open to a two-page spread, filled with morbid illustrations of victims being brutalized.

Except that all the pictures were missing.

Kathleen drew her breath in slowly. She ran her fingers over the mutilated pages, and felt the chill deepen within her.

Who would do such a thing . . . and why?

She picked up the next book.

The Inferno, by Dante.

Someone had left a bookmark stuck between the pages. Her hands trembled as she worked the bookmark free.

It was a torn slip of paper. A slender strip of white paper with words on it, printed in neat black letters.

HORRORS AWAIT YOU. BEWARE.

Books by Richie Tankersley Cusick

BUFFY, THE VAMPIRE SLAYER
(a novelization based on a screenplay by Joss Whedon)
THE DRIFTER
FATAL SECRETS
HELP WANTED
THE LOCKER
THE MALL
OVERDUE
SILENT STALKER
SOMEONE AT THE DOOR
VAMPIRE

Available from ARCHWAY PAPERBACKS

RICHIE TANKERSLEY CUSICK

OVERDUE

AN ARCHWAY PAPERBACK
Published by POCKET BOOKS
New York   London   Toronto   Sydney   Tokyo   Singapore

This book is a work of fiction. Names, characters, places and incidents are products of the author's imagination or are used fictitiously. Any resemblance to actual events or locales or persons, living or dead, is entirely coincidental.

An ARCHWAY PAPERBACK *Original*

An Archway Paperback published by
POCKET BOOKS, a division of Simon & Schuster Inc.
1230 Avenue of the Americas, New York, NY 10020.

ISBN: 0-671-88743-2

First Archway Paperback printing April 1995

10 9 8 7 6 5 4 3 2 1

AN ARCHWAY PAPERBACK and colophon are registered trademarks of Simon & Schuster Inc.

Cover art by Gerber Studio

Printed in the U.S.A.

IL: 6+

for Jane
  spaniels freakin'
  rosehill speakin'
  penboys scowlin'
  geen a-prowlin'
  manuscript-that-makes-me-crazy blues . . .
    invisible buddy o'mine

OVERDUE

Fremont Public Library sat in the ugliest section of town . . . a huge, foreboding structure rising darkly beneath low overhangs of twisted oaks and maples. Having survived the steady and relentless march of time, it was now the oldest building in town, and the one Kathleen hated most. Along with its high-ceilinged rooms and creaky wooden floors, it had taken on a permanent smell of dust and mildew that always made her feel as if she were suffocating. Even on the sunniest of days, the library was as cold and damp as a tomb.

But today hadn't been sunny, nor had it been particularly warm, and Kathleen stood morosely at the window, shivering a little and staring out at the pouring rain.

She despised working here.

Especially toward closing time, when almost everyone else had gone home. Except for Miss

Finch, of course. Miss Finch was always the last to leave, the only one who ever locked up.

"Kathleen?"

The librarian's sharp voice cut through the heavy silence, and Kathleen jumped. The place was so spooky at night. Quiet and musty and full of shadows.

"Yes, Miss Finch?"

"Don't forget to finish shelving the books on that table."

"Yes, Miss Finch."

"And hurry up. It's nearly seven."

Kathleen frowned. From the corner of her eye she could see Robin leaning in the doorway with his broom. He gave a quick, sidelong glance as Miss Finch hurried back to the main room and left them there alone.

Kathleen sighed. "I hate this job, you know that, Robin?"

The janitor nodded. He was seventeen—the same age as she was—but with his silky hair, huge dark eyes, and waifish face, he could pass for someone much younger. Kathleen looked at him now and felt herself smile. Robin could always make her smile. He was only an inch taller than she—shorter than the other guys she knew, and slightly built—and he was also extremely shy. He never spoke, except with his eyes. She'd always heard that a childhood accident had left him mute, but though some of the kids made fun of him and called him slow, Kathleen knew better. He read more books than anyone she'd ever known, and though he'd never finished school, she was willing

2

to bet he was smarter than all the kids at Fremont High.

"I really hate this job," she said again, but more to herself this time than to him. "You want to run away with me, Robin? Start a new life together in some big city somewhere?"

Robin looked amused. The corners of his lips moved in a faint smile.

"You wouldn't like living with me, though," she went on, sliding some books onto a shelf. "I can be really cranky and hard to get along with."

He shook his head and started sweeping. They always had these one-sided conversations when Kathleen was working, and she looked forward to them as the bright spot of her day. Sort of like therapy, she reasoned and grabbed more books from the table as she wandered down another tall row of shelves.

"Do you realize we have the only librarian in the world who's probably older than our library?" she went on. "Which is pretty amazing, since this place has been here over a hundred years." She scanned a row of encyclopedias, then added, "Maybe she'll retire this year. I mean, she *must* know everyone wants to get rid of her. Then we could donate her to the historical society."

She heard the stiff rustle of Robin's broom. Thunder growled in the distance, and from the front desk Miss Finch's muffled voice answered the telephone.

Everyone made fun of Miss Finch; rumors about her had been flying around Fremont for years. Ever since Kathleen could remember, Miss Finch had lived alone without family or friends, and she'd always looked exactly the same—stern and cold and mean. Nobody was really sure how old Miss Finch was, either—but Kathleen had heard her father say many times that Miss Finch was probably younger than she looked, that people shouldn't judge her so harshly, that you just never knew what happened in other people's lives that made them turn out the way they did.

Some speculated that Miss Finch had been jilted by a lover in her younger days, which had left her bitter and angry for life; others said she was really a spy, relocated here to Fremont as part of a witness-protection plan. Kathleen's favorite was that Miss Finch ate small children for breakfast.

"Things aren't any better at home." Kathleen sighed and changed the subject. "I knew you were dying to know. Divorce is the worst, Robin, believe me. I hardly ever see Dad—I think he's trying to lose himself in his work. And when I do hear from Mom, she's still mad because I wouldn't go with her."

She shoved some books into place, then peeked around the end of the aisle at his back.

"And how's my social life, you ask? Always the friend, never the girlfriend, as usual. I'm so glad it's spring break. That new girl at school—Monica Franklin? She's only been here a few weeks, and the guys don't notice anyone else. She's blond and tall and *very* beautiful. So naturally I hate her guts."

Robin paused and turned to face her. He tilted his head quizzically and sketched a dollar sign in the air with his fingertips.

"What?" Kathleen frowned. "Oh—you mean, is

4

she rich? I'll say. She moved into one of those houses by the lake—you know, out where Vivian Wenner's family lives? Her father's a doctor—a plastic surgeon, I think. *And* they have servants."

Kathleen turned away, feeling depressed. She dragged a stepstool down another aisle and climbed up, trying to reach the top shelf.

"Monica latched on to Vivian the first day she started school," Kathleen went on. "As if *that's* any big surprise. Now they do everything together. They both act like they own the whole school and everyone should worship them."

With a groan Kathleen heaved the last of the books up into place.

"I always thought I'd be able to get away from Vivian and her clones once I graduate. I mean, just yesterday everyone was talking about college and where they're going this fall. But now . . . with the divorce and everything . . ."

She leaned her forehead against the edge of the shelf and took a deep breath.

"Isn't this sad, Robin? Spring break's just starting, everyone has these exotic trips planned, and I'm stuck here in the library. So what do you think, am I horrible? I know I shouldn't care about all this stupid stuff, but sometimes I can't help it. I don't *really* want to be like Monica or Vivian. . . . Well . . . okay, so I wouldn't mind having a perfect face like Monica—but who wouldn't?"

Exasperated with herself, Kathleen climbed down from the stool and started back between the tall, narrow rows of books.

"Robin?" She sighed. "Okay, I know I'm babbling, so forget what I said. Just forget all about—"

Kathleen broke off and stared. All this time she'd thought the two of them were alone, but as she rounded the corner of the aisle, she was just in time to see a tall shadow slipping through the doorway on the far wall.

"Robin?" her voice rose. "Robin, where are you?"

She didn't hear the broom anymore . . . she didn't hear anything at all. *That's just great. . . . If it was someone from school, they were probably listening to everything I said.* She cringed just thinking about what would happen at school if her offhand remarks were spread around. The wrath of Vivian and Monica wasn't something she particularly looked forward to.

Kathleen hurried to the door and crept nervously into the adjoining room. She still couldn't hear anything—not the shuffle of feet or the sliding of books or even the creaking of floorboards. Moving quickly along the ends of the aisles, she scanned each one as she passed, then hesitated, her eyes darting between two more connecting doorways. One led off to more rooms at the rear of the building, the other to the checkout area in front. Kathleen chose the second and stepped over the threshold into the main part of the library.

Miss Finch was still on the phone. The front door was just swinging shut from outside. A small group of lingering readers was clustered around the desk waiting to be checked out, but they all had their backs to her, they all wore coats, and from where she stood, they all seemed reasonably tall.

Kathleen bit her lip and grasped the edge of the doorframe. *You're being silly—none of the kids*

*from school ever come to this library if they can help
it—and especially not on break. And even if they
did, and they heard you talking, what can you do
about it now?*

A hand closed over her arm, and she jumped,
choking back a yell.

"Robin!" Kathleen hissed. "Don't do that—you
scared me to death!"

He touched her shoulder lightly, a gesture of
apology. Then he turned back toward the room
he'd been cleaning, and Kathleen reluctantly followed.

"Where'd you go?" she asked him. "I thought
you were there, and I was talking the whole time."

He took his broom from the corner, and
Kathleen eased down into a chair, watching him
sweep.

"Did you see anyone else in here a minute ago?"
she asked.

Robin raised an eyebrow. His gaze traveled slowly from one end of the room to the other, then
settled back on her.

Kathleen groaned. "I didn't know anyone else
was in here with us. And I was going on and on,
saying all those mean things—"

"Kathleen?" Miss Finch yelled. There was a firm
and final slam of the front door. "Don't forget
those books for the auction! Have Robin carry the
boxes out to my car. And tell him to be careful!"

"He's not deaf, Miss Finch," Kathleen muttered,
but aloud she called back, "Okay, I'll tell him!"

Exchanging grins, she and Robin made their way
through the other rooms on the first floor. Years ago
the place had been a private home, and the kitchen

7

at the back was still used for coffee breaks and meetings, deliveries, cleaning supplies, and general storage. Kathleen surveyed the cartons strewn across the linoleum floor and slowly shook her head.

"They look heavy," she said. "Did you move all these yourself?"

As Robin nodded, she walked over to the back door and frowned.

"Oh, this is great. Look—she's left it open, and it's raining in through the screen door. As if this place wasn't damp enough already. Okay, let me pull her car in closer so we won't have so far to carry."

She let herself out onto the porch, squinting against the rain, stepping carefully over scraps of old lumber, paintcans, and pieces of broken flowerpots. A single bulb sputtered weakly from the roof overhead; other than that and the glow from the kitchen, there was no light out here at all. A narrow alleyway ran between the back of the building and the high stone wall opposite, where thick tangles of trees bent groundward, branches whipping fiercely in the wind. Kathleen heard the door creak open and felt Robin's presence, warm and calm beside her.

"I don't like this," she murmured. "I think the rain's getting worse."

To her surprise, Robin's hand slid to her arm. His fingers began to squeeze, and she could feel the slow, hard tensing of his muscles. As Kathleen glanced at him in alarm, she saw his eyes fixed on the darkness ahead.

"What is it?" she asked. "What's wrong?"

He shook his head. His grip tightened, and he took a step forward. For a split second Kathleen was afraid to breathe. She watched as his gaze climbed steadily from the stone wall to the tree-tops, to the black, churning sky.

"Robin?" Kathleen whispered.

Without warning he shoved her back. In the exact same instant a huge explosion sounded, and one of the trees crackled with silver light and began to fall.

"Robin!" Kathleen stared in awe as the tree toppled in slow motion, crashing at one end of the driveway. "How'd you know that was going to happen?"

She tugged on his hand, but he wouldn't move. As a gust of wind drenched them with rain, he pulled from her grasp and lifted his arm to keep her back.

"Come on," she pleaded. "Let's go in before something else happens."

But she could feel his uneasiness, and a cold stab of fear went through her as she quickly scanned their surroundings. Trees and shadows merged together beyond reach of the light. Rain fell harder, and thunder vibrated the flimsy boards beneath their feet.

"Robin—" Kathleen began, then stopped.

For just a second she thought she'd seen something through the downpour near the wall. Something other than flailing branches and tall dead grass and scattering piles of leaves . . .

Something dark and furtive and very, very silent,

crouched far back beyond the low sweep of trees and shadows. . . .

"What was that?" Kathleen whispered. "Did you see it?"

Robin said nothing, of course.

But his hand closed firmly on her arm as he steered her back inside.

2

Can you take care of the library for me, Kathleen?" Miss Finch asked. "I know it's spring break and you probably have lots of other plans. But it seems I *must* attend this librarian's seminar, and I've just found out about it this evening. Frankly, I'm beside myself."

Kathleen watched as Miss Finch paced back and forth across the kitchen floor. Her stomach felt queasy, and she rubbed her forehead while a thousand excuses whirled through her brain.

"I'm not sure, Miss Finch, I'd have to check at home and—"

"Oh. Yes." Miss Finch stopped, her lips pursed. "How thoughtless of me. How *is* your situation at home, Kathleen?"

"Mom's still gone, if that's what you mean. Dad's really busy." A stab of unhappiness shot through her, and she groped for something to say.

11

"I've got my friends. You know . . . we're okay. Thanks for asking."

"Of course." A quick, tight-lipped smile. "Well. Under ordinary circumstances, I wouldn't put *anyone* in charge of my library," Miss Finch went on. "You know that. But you're the *only* one I'd trust." She stopped and stared at the kitchen floor. "Why aren't these boxes in my car?"

"He's going to do it when you leave, Miss Finch," Kathleen said quickly. "It was raining so hard, we were afraid everything would be soaked."

She and Robin exchanged glances. Miss Finch cast a critical eye toward the window.

"Yes, it is nasty out there," she relented. "But don't forget, Robin—I still have to drop the boxes off at the school this evening. I'm counting on those books to bring in a lot of money for our new children's room."

Robin nodded.

"About my predicament, Kathleen," Miss Finch tried again, and when Kathleen hesitated, the librarian faced her with a loud sigh. "It's very *important*, naturally, or I'd never impose. I'll be leaving tomorrow, so it's imperative you're here in the morning to get my keys."

She fumbled the keyring from her purse, waving it in front of Kathleen's nose.

"You will guard these with your life. My library is a sanctuary and haven. A sacred place." She drew a deep breath, eyes filling her bifocals. "And tomorrow is Thursday, don't forget—*late* night."

As if Kathleen could forget. It was bad enough working regular evenings, much less on Thursdays when the library stayed open till nine. She looked over at Robin washing his hands at the sink. His head was lowered, and he looked as if he was trying not to laugh. Swallowing hard, she finally relented.

"Okay. I guess I can."

"Excellent. Oh, and one more thing," Miss Finch said crisply, dropping the keys back into her purse. "Robin, I picked up some more paint for the new room. If you could get it from my car, please? I expect to see a *lot* of progress made by the time I get back."

"But Miss Finch," Kathleen spoke up for him as Robin turned in surprise from the sink. "It'll take months to get that room in shape! Painting's the least of the problems. The walls have to be patched —there's all those mildew stains—most of the floor has to be pulled up—and that awful ceiling— and the shelves have to be moved—and the—"

"Don't tell *me,* Kathleen, tell Robin. He's the one doing all the work." Miss Finch sounded annoyed. "Now, don't dawdle. I have to lock up."

Again Robin and Kathleen exchanged looks. Kathleen put on her coat and tucked her long brown hair inside the collar. "Any special instructions?" she asked the librarian reluctantly.

"Just be here on time tomorrow. I left a list in my desk drawer. There's lots of work for you to do, so you won't want to waste any time."

Kathleen sighed. "I'll be here."

She waved at Robin and followed Miss Finch to the main room. Miss Finch was big on routines, and this one never varied. She would let Kathleen out, wait to see that she reached the sidewalk, and lock the front door. Then she'd turn out the lights, room by room, leaving the lamp on behind the front desk. Then she and Robin would go out the back, and she'd ask Robin to wait while she got in her car and locked all her doors. She didn't like anyone being in the library after she left, so Robin never stayed past closing time. He cleaned up throughout the day so he could go home when everyone else did.

"Good night, Kathleen," Miss Finch said. "Be careful, and give my best to your father."

Kathleen got her umbrella open and started toward the street. At the corner she turned and waved, then watched the door close and the windows go dark. She wished she had a car so she could give Robin a ride home. He didn't have transportation, either, and he lived farther away than she did, on the opposite end of town.

For a moment she huddled there in the downpour, narrowing her eyes at the library. It loomed far back from the sidewalk, all alone in its weed-grown lot. A wet gust of March wind scattered dead leaves across the pavement. Gnarled tree limbs clawed at the old stone walls, and one front window began to glow a murky shade of gray.

The car horn startled her.

Looking back at the street, she saw the headlights skidding toward the curb, and she barely managed to jump out of the way in time.

"Kathleen!" a voice shouted. "Is that you? Wait a minute!"

The car squealed to a stop beneath the street lamp. As the window eased down on the driver's side, Kathleen saw a long cascade of platinum blond hair and stepped back with a scowl.

"My goodness, Kathleen! You look like a drowned rat!"

The blond girl giggled and leaned slightly out the window. She shook the curls back from her flawless complexion and flashed a perfect smile. The rain didn't even touch her. It wouldn't dare, Kathleen supposed.

"Monica. How nice of you to point that out," Kathleen retorted blandly.

"What are you doing here?" Monica went on, glancing around at the deserted street. "I've heard this isn't a part of town to be in after dark."

Kathleen made a vague motion. "The library," she said. "And you're a long way from home."

"These stupid books . . ." Monica gave a long-suffering sigh. "I needed them for speech class and they're due back today—as if I don't have anything better to do. Vivian and I have to start packing—we're leaving for the beach on Saturday."

Like I care, Kathleen thought, but aloud she said, "The library's closed."

"Oh, that's right—you work here! No wonder you make such good grades, Kathleen. You don't ever go out, do you—just work and study, and study and work."

"My life is just so dull." Kathleen's smile was sickeningly sweet, but Monica rushed on.

"You know, I was just wondering how Bran is. I mean, he must be really sick—no one saw him at school the last few days. In fact, I heard"—her lips curled suggestively—"he's been spending a lot of time in bed."

Kathleen stared back tightly.

"I thought if *anyone* would know about that"— Monica shrugged—*"you* would."

Kathleen took a deep breath. Somehow she managed to keep her voice level. "He's got the flu."

"Oh, what a shame." Monica pouted. "I *really* miss him."

"I bet."

"In fact, just today I was talking to Viv about him . . . wondering how I could cheer him up." She frowned and twirled one strand of hair around a perfectly manicured nail. "You know, I get the feeling Viv's really serious about Bran. Like maybe she wants him all to herself?"

Kathleen shifted her umbrella as she wiped raindrops from her face. "Well, Bran's not serious about Vivian."

"Really?" Monica's face brightened. "Like . . . Bran doesn't *belong* to her?"

In spite of herself Kathleen laughed. "Bran doesn't belong to anybody. They've gone out a few times, but that's it. At least as far as I know."

"And you know everything about Bran, don't you?" Monica's eyes narrowed slyly. "I hear you two are really . . . *really* close."

Kathleen hesitated. She stared at Monica's fake smile and tried to keep her voice level.

"Friends," she said at last. "We're good friends."

"That's sweet," Monica purred. "Well . . . maybe you can help me, then. See, I'd like to call Bran and tell him how much I've been thinking about him—just to cheer him up, you know. But the thing is"—her expression changed to total bewilderment—"Vivian said she didn't know his phone number, and I can't find it in the phone book and—"

"It's unlisted," Kathleen said shortly. "I have to go."

"Oh, but, Kathleen, surely you must know his—"

"If you want Bran's number, you'll have to ask *him* for it," Kathleen repeated stubbornly. "See you."

"Well, aren't you the little watchdog," Monica simpered.

Without warning she tossed some books at Kathleen. Instinctively Kathleen grabbed for them but missed, and the books landed in a puddle at her feet.

Monica smiled. "You don't mind taking these for me, do you, Kathleen? I mean, since the library's closed and you *do* work there, after all, and I'm already late."

She lifted her arm in a careless wave. Kathleen stood there in the rain and watched as the car wheeled around and sped off down the street. *Don't offer me a ride or anything, I'm only drowning here.* She pulled her coat tighter, picked up the wet books, and automatically reached for her shoulder. *My purse. I forgot my stupid purse.*

Groaning, Kathleen sloshed back through the dripping trees up to the library's wide front porch. Light showed faintly beyond the beveled glass of the door, and she tugged on the handle.

"Miss Finch! Robin! Let me in—I forgot my purse!"

She pressed her ear against the door, listening. No sound came from inside. She tried the knob again, but the door stuck fast.

"Miss Finch! Open up! Oh, this is just great."

Kicking the door, she turned to leave. Without warning it popped open behind her, and as she spun back around, a blast of wind slammed it into the wall. Kathleen made a grab for it and lunged inside. She finally managed to wrestle it shut, then stood for a moment, catching her breath, slowly scanning the empty room.

"Miss Finch?"

It was as silent as a tomb.

Shadows gathered noiselessly into corners . . . oozed between high, narrow rows of shelves. They wove among the tables and chairs and old wooden card files and lay along the front desk piled high with books. One lamp burned softly behind the counter, casting a murky haze across the floorboards, and the black, stormy skies beyond the uncurtained windows only intensified the gloom.

Kathleen cleared her throat. She swallowed several times before she spoke.

"Miss Finch?" she called again. She took a hesitant step forward . . . glanced back over her shoulder. Even the silence was dank and musty. "Miss—"

The noise stopped her.

Catching her breath, Kathleen sensed, rather than saw, a movement on the far side of the room. A slight shifting of darkness . . . as though something had pulled out of sight behind the bookshelves in the corner.

A slow, cold shiver went up her spine.

"Miss Finch?" she murmured. "Robin? Is that you?"

Thunder rattled the windowpanes . . . shook the floor beneath her feet. As lightning split the sky, shadows lurched around her, and the walls seemed to ripple from ceiling to floor. For one split second she could have sworn she heard the faint, faint sound of whispering. . . .

"Miss Finch?"

And her own voice was barely a whisper now as she inched toward the door, ears straining through the eerie silence. To her dismay, the knob was stuck again, and after several futile tries, she gave up and turned back to her surroundings. Empty doorways gaped at her from every side; to the right of the desk a staircase rose up into darkness.

Don't panic. Just go to the kitchen and find your purse and call Miss Finch at home. Then she can come back and lock up after you again.

She was almost positive her purse was in the kitchen. She'd probably left it in the closet where she'd hung her coat. Kathleen stared at the door on the right-hand wall. She'd have to go through there—and through several more doors beyond that—to reach the kitchen. And there was no central control for the lights—she'd have to feel along the walls as she went through each dark room. . . .

A rumble of thunder echoed in the distance; rain beat heavily against the roof. From some uneasy corner of her mind she was halfway conscious of water dripping. Her eyes lifted to the ugly stains across the ceiling, but with all the shadows it was impossible to tell what was leaking.

Lightning burst beyond the windowpanes. For a split second Kathleen could see the tree falling again behind the library, and Robin staring and staring out into the night. Then she remembered the strange shadows in the alleyway, and Robin's grip on her arm as he'd forced her back inside.

Robin . . . what was that . . . did you see it, too?

And suddenly she was afraid—afraid to stay here, afraid to go back out in the dark. Trying to stay calm, she forced herself to walk to the desk and pick up the telephone.

She knew the number as well as her own. She dialed, then waited for him to answer.

One ring. Two.

Nervously she shifted from one foot to the other, eyes scanning the shadows. Three rings . . . four . . .

"Come on, Bran, pick up. . . ."

She set the books down on the counter. Six rings. Eight. At last she heard a click and a staticky burst of music on the other end of the line. Then a sleepy voice mumbled, "H'lo?"

Kathleen went weak with relief. "Bran, I need you."

For a moment he didn't speak. She could picture him, all drowsy and confused, staring at the phone, trying to wake up. "You do?" he said at last. "Who is this?"

"Me, you idiot! It's an emergency!"

"Kath, I'm sick!"

"And I'm stranded here!"

"Where's here?"

"The library. I'm sort of locked in."

"What do you mean, *sorta* locked in? How can you be *sorta* locked—"

"Bran!" Kathleen's voice rose. "I'm really scared!"

"Why? What's wrong?"

"I'm not sure. Please come and get me."

The background music faded, then shut off. Bran made a sound halfway between a sigh and a groan.

"Tell me my phone didn't really ring just now. Tell me this whole conversation is just my cold medicine—"

"Bran, I'm serious! I've got to get out of here!"

"So get out. Every door and window can't be locked—"

"I don't want to go outside by myself!"

Another pause. Another groan.

"Okay, okay," he grumbled. "Just let me get some clothes on—"

"Hurry!" Kathleen glanced over her shoulder. The shadows seemed thicker somehow, as if they'd gathered and crept closer while she wasn't looking. "Please—oh, no . . ."

"Kath?" Bran asked uncertainly. "Kath, what is it?"

"I—I'm not sure," she stammered. "I thought . . . I thought I heard something."

"Something? Something what?"

"I don't know. The door, maybe—"

"I'm on my way."

21

She heard him slam the phone down. She stood with the telephone clutched in her hand, staring at the front door.

Had the knob turned just then? Or was it just a play of shadows as lightning flashed beyond the windows?

Slowly she replaced the receiver. She rubbed the chill from her arms and started cautiously toward the door. She didn't hear anything now . . . nothing but the wind and the rain and the ominous growl of thunder. *Oh, Bran . . . please hurry. . . .*

She stopped several feet from the door. Her eyes moved over the beveled glass at the top . . . down again to the doorknob. She stared at the floor, and then suddenly, helplessly, she laughed.

The book drop.

While she'd been on the phone panicking, someone had come by, found the library closed for the night, and shoved their books through the slot in the outside wall. Now as Kathleen bent to retrieve them, she drew a deep, shaky breath to steady herself. Her knees felt like rubber. She carried the books back to the desk and turned up the lamp. Might as well check them in while she waited for Bran to come and rescue her.

I can't tell him about this, that's for sure. I'll never hear the end of it.

There was quite a stack. Kathleen shrugged out of her coat and sat down at the counter. Five good-sized volumes. Someone who liked to read, obviously, yet Kathleen felt a chill as she began sorting through the subject matter. Death. Murder. Executions. One by one, she placed the books

22

aside, her apprehension growing. Who on earth would check out such grisly topics?

She picked up another one—an encyclopedia of torture—and turned to the back, looking for the due date. To her surprise, the last date stamped there was over six months old. Puzzled, she went through the ones she'd already set aside, but those dates, too, had been stamped months earlier. *Which means either these books are way overdue— or someone sneaked them out.*

Intrigued now, Kathleen went to the files. It was easy to find the names of all the people who'd last checked out the books—and according to library records, all those same books had been turned in again on time.

Kathleen sat back in her chair. She rubbed one hand along her forehead, her brow furrowed in thought. It was pretty obvious now that whoever had just returned these books had never intended to do it in daylight.

Once more she turned her attention to the volume on torture. She started to turn the front cover, but to her surprise, the book fell open and lay flat on the desk. Looking closely, Kathleen could see how the spine was creased, as though whoever had been reading it had come back to this particular section again and again and again. . . .

It was a two-page spread, filled with morbid illustrations of victims being brutalized . . .

Except that all the pictures were missing.

Kathleen drew her breath in slowly. She ran her fingers over the mutilated pages and felt the chill deepen within her.

The captions were still there, labeling each depiction of pain and agony. But where the illustrations should have been, there were only jagged holes, as though someone had hacked them out with scissors.

Who would do such a thing . . . and why?

She skimmed through several more chapters. Again the book fell open to a section of gruesome illustrations; again each one had been slashed and removed. *Not the kind of stuff you'd want to put in a scrapbook,* she thought wryly and shoved the book aside.

There was one left. As Kathleen picked it up, she saw that it was different from the others, and she read the title out loud.

"Inferno. By Dante."

She was familiar with it, of course. It had been assigned reading in her special advanced lit class—a ponderous narration of the author's journey through hell in search of paradise—and not one of her particular favorites. She ran her fingers over the clothbound cover and leaned closer. Someone had left a bookmark stuck between the pages, about halfway through. She started to pull it out, then suddenly froze.

Something creaked behind her.

Softly . . . softly . . . very close by . . .

Whirling in her chair, Kathleen scanned the shadows with frightened eyes. A burst of lightning sputtered faintly at the window, then plunged the room into darkness once more.

She hadn't realized she'd been holding her breath. Now she let it out slowly and sagged back in her chair.

OVERDUE

She stared down at the book in front of her. Her hands trembled as she worked the bookmark free.

It was only a torn slip of paper. A slender strip of white paper with words on it, printed in neat black letters.

The message was clear. And yet it took her several minutes before she could fully grasp the meaning. . . .

HORRORS AWAIT YOU. BEWARE.

Kathleen jumped up and ran for the door.

"Bran!" she called. "Bran, get me out of here!"

The handle stuck fast. Frantically she twisted and pulled, until suddenly the door flew open, sending sheets of rain across the library floor.

"Hey! What's going on in there!"

With a scream Kathleen stepped back. She saw the tall figure framed there in the doorway, and as she prepared to run, it started coming slowly toward her.

Lightning crashed, flooding the room with eerie yellow light. The stranger reached behind him and slammed the door shut.

"You!" he said angrily. "Come over here!"

Kathleen got ready to scream again. She opened her mouth, but suddenly he grabbed her, his hand smothering her cries.

"Stop that!" He gave her a shake. "I hate screaming."

26

She tried to free herself, but he only held her tighter, his body pressed firmly against her own. She twisted her head and felt his hand clamp harder over her mouth.

"Don't," he said. "I'm not going to hurt you."

This time she stopped fighting. As a wave of dizziness washed over her, she nodded to show she understood.

She could feel him hesitating. At last his hand slid from her face and he stepped back, and Kathleen wobbled sideways, taking deep gulps of air.

"What do you want!" she gasped. "Who *are* you?"

"Alexander," he said without the slightest hesitation. To her dismay he held out his hand for her to shake. "Hodges. The third."

Kathleen stared. She dropped her eyes to his hand, and then raised them again to his face.

"What?"

"Alexander Hodges the third," he repeated calmly. "But you can call me Alexander. Are you all right?"

Confusion and anger churned inside her. She fought off a second wave of dizziness and narrowed her eyes, her voice tight.

"Where did you *come* from?"

"California," he said.

Kathleen glowered at him. He shrugged and cleared his throat.

"Oh, you mean just now?" He lifted his arm, motioning toward the door. "Outside. I heard all the yelling and . . ." He stopped, looking her up and down. "I thought the library was closed."

Kathleen took another deep breath, not trusting herself to speak. She was still shaking, and she hugged her arms around her chest so he wouldn't notice.

"It *is* closed," she said finally, between clenched teeth.

"So what's all the commotion?" he asked. "I thought someone needed help, but obviously—"

"I happen to work here."

Again his eyes did a quick survey from her head to her feet. "I see." He glanced around. "Let me guess. You're a night person, and you don't use lights."

"I came back to get my purse. That's all."

"Which still doesn't explain all the yelling."

"I . . ." She hugged herself tighter. "I'm fine. It was a mistake."

"Oh. Well. That's a relief. And you are . . . ?"

"Never mind who I am. Did you put some books in the book drop just now?" she asked suspiciously, but his look was blank.

"Book drop?"

"Yes. By the front door."

"No. As a matter of fact, I've never used this library before. I was coming here to get acquainted."

"Why?"

"Excuse me." He arched a brow at her. "Do I need to fill out a questionnaire before I can read in this place?"

Kathleen glared. Abruptly she put her back to him and concentrated on the front window.

"Of course not. I was just wondering why you

were out there if the library's closed. You shouldn't *be* out there if the library's closed."

"Yes, ma'am."

Now he sounded as if he was trying not to laugh, and Kathleen turned back toward him. As he lowered his head, a narrow shaft of lightning lit up the window, throwing his face in and out of shadow. He was probably six feet tall, dressed in tight jeans and a black turtleneck sweater. He had a strong chin, rather pointed, and chiseled features that were almost stern—yet his mouth looked soft and sensual, and behind wire-rimmed glasses, his deep blue eyes gazed back at her with intense calm. Dark brows rested low over his eyes, and his black hair was combed straight back from the widow's peak at the top of his high forehead.

"So you came back for your purse," Alexander's voice interrupted her silent appraisal. "And then you started yelling, but it was a mistake."

He was watching her, and she felt stupid. Grudgingly she said, "The door was stuck. I thought I was locked in."

He considered this a moment. Finally he said, "You know . . . people don't usually panic like that when they get locked inside a place they work." He waited for Kathleen to answer. When she didn't, he added, "It sounded to me more like something was after you."

Kathleen flushed. She dropped her eyes and tried to think of something clever to say. The silence grew longer. . . . It was Alexander who finally spoke again.

"Look, I'm sorry if I scared you. I meant well."

Another explosion of lightning. Kathleen jumped, then quickly looked away.

"Scared of storms?" Alexander asked her.

"Of course not."

"Just libraries?"

She dropped her eyes and shrugged. "I don't like libraries."

"All libraries? Or just this library?"

"All libraries. But *especially* this library. They're quiet and stuffy. And creepy."

Alexander sighed, letting his gaze travel slowly around the room. "I have to admit, I never expected anything quite . . . well . . . quite like this."

"You're obviously not from a small town."

"Really, does it show?"

She ignored the sarcasm. "When you were outside, did you see anyone else out front?" She tried to keep her voice casual, but a twinge of fear crept in. "Just a few minutes ago? By the front door?"

"If I answer, will you tell me your name?"

She hesitated, then let out an exasperated sigh. "Kathleen. Did you see anyone?"

"No. Why?"

"No cars parked on the street . . . or people on the sidewalk? Anyone . . . you know . . . hanging around?"

Alexander studied her taut expression, then said carefully, "No cars, no people. No one. So what's all this about the book drop?"

"What are you doing here, anyway?" she hurried on, throwing a quick glance at the front desk. "You still haven't said why you're—"

"Ah, so I *do* have to fill out a questionnaire."

"Of course not." She flushed. "I was just wondering, that's all. Nobody around here comes to the library this late."

"You *got* me," he put his hands up in mock surrender. "I'm an outsider. All the way from Brookside."

Kathleen almost smiled at that. Brookside was a neighboring town, all of forty miles away. "You're from the university?" she guessed, and Alexander nodded.

"History major. And for all this quaint and cozy atmosphere," he deadpanned, indicating the room in general, "your little library here has quite a reputation for regional history and folklore, am I right?"

"Yes. The best collection in the county."

"That's" why I'm here."

Kathleen nodded slowly. "So you're doing a paper or something?"

"Term paper. I've been through everything in the university library. I thought I'd see what I could find around here."

"Well, you can't check out any of the books," Kathleen told him. She wished he'd just leave. She wished Bran would show up so she could get out of here. "They're all in a special room upstairs."

"A special room," he repeated. He cocked his head and gave her a quizzical look. "Can I work right there in that special room?"

"Of course you can," she said impatiently. "The library's open from ten to seven. Nine on Thursdays, five on Saturdays, four on Sundays."

"And will you be working here?" he asked.

The question surprised her. She glanced over and saw him smile.

"I *said* I worked here, didn't I?" she grumbled.

"How old are you? No, let me guess—junior? Senior?"

"I'm a senior," she said irritably. "Not that it's any of your business."

"Then shouldn't you be on spring break now?" He narrowed his eyes and calmly appraised her. "Long brown hair . . . what—brown eyes?" He squinted and leaned closer. "Yes, brown eyes. . . . You're a small thing, aren't you? Short and tiny— so how come you're not off somewhere on a wild holiday with your tall, tan boyfriend?"

Kathleen flushed deeply. "Don't tell me what I look like, I know what I look like, thank you very much." As a smile played at the corners of Alexander's mouth, her face reddened even more. "Now, listen," she said angrily, "I told you the library's closed, and you shouldn't even be here, so would you please—"

She broke off as something pounded frantically at the door.

"Kath!" a voice shouted. "Hey, Kath, you in there?"

Alexander shot her a curious glance as the door burst open and another gust of wind swept in, driving rain and dead leaves and a bedraggled figure halfway across the floor.

"Bran!" Kathleen gave a sigh of relief. "What took you so long?"

"Sorry—Ma wouldn't let me leave. At least not till I told her I was coming after you." He took her arm and looked her quickly up and down. "You okay?"

"Yes, but—"

"What happened?"

"I'll tell you later."

"But you're *okay.*"

"Yes, yes, I'm fine."

"Geez, Kath, you scared the shit out of me."

He was so cute. It was all she could do not to hug him, but she knew it would only make him mad. She could tell he'd rushed to come over, because nothing he was wearing matched, and his jacket was turned inside out. He was soaking wet and looked exhausted, but even in the throes of the flu, Bran was irresistible. Every girl at Fremont High— from freshman to seniors—wished Bran Vanelli would ask them for a date. The fact that Kathleen was his friend and had known him for years made her rather an object of envy in their eyes—but to her, Bran was always just Bran.

Watching him struggle to shut the door, Kathleen had to smile. He was tall and thin, and his clothes always hung a little too loose on his lanky frame. His shoulder-length brown hair was parted in the middle and pushed back behind his ears, revealing high, tight cheekbones, a not so delicate nose, and a quick smile that was warm and genuine. He had a dark olive complexion and just the slightest dimple in his left cheek, and brown eyes that always looked sad, even though he seldom was.

"So I didn't need to come after all? Is that what you're telling me?" His voice had always been scratchy, but his cold only made it worse. "Thanks, Kath, I really wasn't miserable enough an hour ago." His face wrinkled up, and he sneezed. "I really *wanted* pneumonia, okay?"

He hadn't noticed they weren't alone. But now as

he came farther into the room, Bran squinted toward the wall and saw Alexander.

"So what's going on?" he asked. "How come you're here in the dark? With some guy?"

"That's Alexander," Kathleen corrected him. "Hodges the third."

"Wow, a title." As Bran considered this, his face lit with a slow smile. "Yeah, okay, I'm impressed."

Before Kathleen could stop him, he ambled over and introduced himself. The boys exchanged pleasantries, then turned their attention on her. There was a long, awkward silence.

"Well," Alexander said at last. "I should be going."

"Yes, you should. Goodbye." Kathleen nearly pushed him out the door as Bran looked on in surprise.

In the threshold Alexander paused and glanced back. "So how come the tall, tan boyfriend's not taking you anywhere?

"He's not my boyfriend," Kathleen retorted indignantly. "Goodbye!"

This time she did manage to push him out and locked the door after him. Bran stood there regarding her with a frown.

"Was he talking about me?" he asked her.

"Yes. Just forget about it."

"He thought I was your boyfriend?"

"He was just making small talk."

"Well, you didn't have to sound so disgusted about it," Bran said grumpily. "It's an insult to me, too."

"Just forget about it." Kathleen punched him on

the shoulder. "Come here, I want to show you something."

"I crawl out of my deathbed and drive like a maniac to get over here, and I find you and some guy hanging around and having a fine old time."

"Bran!" Kathleen grabbed his arm and shook it. "Will you pay attention? *Please!* Look at these books!"

"What books?" Bran demanded, but Kathleen was already pulling him over to the desk.

"It wasn't *just* the books," she tried to explain. "It was the torture book with all the holes, and then the bookmark with the writing on it."

Bran grunted. "You've always had a way with words, Kath. It's one of your strong points."

"I'm serious!" Kathleen shot daggers at him. "Someone wrote a warning and left it in this book. And cut out a lot of pictures in another book."

Bran gave a low whistle. "Miss Finch'll have a cow."

"Forget Miss Finch." Kathleen picked up each book in turn and shoved it in Bran's face. "Just look at all these weird titles. And whoever brought them back tonight never officially checked them out. Which means he must not have wanted anyone to know he had them in the first place."

"Kath, what are you *talking* about?"

"See this?" Kathleen opened the encyclopedia of torture and slammed it down on the desk. Immediately it fell open to one section of mutilated pages. "Why would someone cut this stuff out? And look here—" Picking up the *Inferno,* she took the bookmark and thrust it at him. "Read it."

Bran did so, then put it down with a sigh. "So? What's your point?"

"My point?" As Kathleen stared at him, Bran nodded.

"Well, yeah. Your point. You're telling me *this* is why I had to run over here in the middle of the night, in the middle of a storm, in the middle of my flu?"

Kathleen looked amazed. "Did you *read* this? Bran, what's the *matter* with you?"

"What's the matter with *you?*" Bran echoed, giving a dry laugh. "Kath, it's a *joke!*"

"A joke?" Kathleen mumbled, but Bran was nodding at her, motioning to the chair, trying to get her to sit down. When she ignored him, he simply pushed her into it.

"Listen to me." He leaned back against the desk and ran his hands back through his wet hair. "Aren't you the one always telling me how kids ruin books? Aren't you always saying how pages get ripped out and you find cartoons and stuff written in there?" When she didn't answer, he spread his arms persuasively. "Those words don't mean anything! They're just words."

"It *could* mean something," Kathleen said stubbornly. "I was here alone, and someone left those books. With that message!"

Bran stared at her, then groaned. "Come on, that's dumb. Somebody just sneaked them back so they wouldn't have to pay a fine. And besides, you don't even know how long that bookmark's been in that book."

Kathleen stared down at the desk, frowning.

"It's probably some jerk doing a term paper,"

Bran went on. "Or . . . you know . . . a book report!" He looked pleased with himself. "Yeah, that's probably it."

"Someone at school?" Kathleen asked nervously.

"Fremont kids aren't the only ones who come here," Bran reminded her. "You got the junior college . . . you got the university an hour away . . ." He stopped, then tried again. "The point is, anyone in town—or out of town, for that matter—could have had these books."

As Kathleen took several more moments to consider this, Bran was seized with a fit of coughing.

"*Now* can we go home? Please?" He looked at her imploringly. "I'd like to die in my own bed."

He started toward the door, but Kathleen stayed put.

"Now what's wrong?" Bran demanded.

She shook her head. She ran her hands over the books and stared at them some more.

"Hey, don't be embarrassed." Bran sauntered back and patted her shoulder. "It's not like this is the first time you've ever done something stupid."

Kathleen brushed his hand away. "My purse," she mumbled. "I've got to find my purse."

"You want me to come with you?"

"*No.*"

"Fine. I'll just stand here and burn up with fever."

While Bran waited by the front door, Kathleen went to the kitchen. As she'd suspected, her purse had fallen from its hook in the closet and was lying on the floor. She picked it up and walked back to the main room, then followed Bran out onto the porch.

"What am I going to do about the door?" she worried. "Miss Finch has the keys."

"Like who'd break into a library?" Bran gave an exaggerated shudder. "All those books around, watching you, with all those big words and stuff."

Kathleen shook her head and slammed the door shut behind them.

A hard rain was still coming down, currents of water flowing swiftly along the curbs. Squinting her eyes, Kathleen looked up and down the dark, narrow street . . . along the empty lots and old, condemned houses . . . through the hazy patches of fog.

"You blew it, Kath," Bran said, taking her purse while she buttoned up her coat.

"Blew what?" she asked distractedly.

"If you hadn't been so pushy with that Alexander guy back there, he might have asked you for a date."

Any other time she would have been ready for battle. But now Kathleen put her hand on his arm and squeezed.

"Take me home, Bran. Now."

"Ouch! Okay, okay, what's the matter with you?"

He glanced at her face, but she didn't see him. Instead her eyes stayed fixed on the shadows, and in spite of her coat, he could feel her shiver.

Instinctively Bran moved closer. "Hey, Kath, cut it out—you're being weirder than usual, okay?"

"But don't you feel it?" she whispered. "Someone's watching us."

4

There you are!" Mrs. Vanelli met them at the kitchen door, wringing her hands, ushering them both inside. "I was ready to call the police! The FBI!"

"Ma"—Bran shot her a look—"stop with the dramatics, okay? Kath's being weird enough for everyone."

"She's a lamb." Mrs. Vanelli caught Kathleen in a huge, warm hug. "A lamb! And *you*"—she glared at Bran over Kathleen's shoulder—"you have *no* sense at all, this girl is so wonderful!"

"She's crazy. She's making me feel creepy."

"You are creepy," Kathleen returned mildly.

"She's being paranoid," Bran went on, as if he hadn't heard. "Thinks people are watching her. Thinks psychos are taking over the library."

"What?" Mrs. Vanelli looked alarmed. "Where can we be safe, if not the library?"

"Forget it, Ma, it's a joke."

"But she's scared, I can see." Mrs. Vanelli shook her head, holding Kathleen at arm's length, looking hard into her face. *"That's* no joke. Take off those wet things and get warm."

Kathleen chuckled in spite of herself. Everything about Bran's mother was larger than life—her size, her voice, her Italian accent, her laugh, and especially her hugs. Now Mrs. Vanelli released her and started pulling her out of her coat.

"You need to eat, *cara,"* she fussed. "It'll make you feel better. I know these things."

"What she *needs* is a psychiatrist," Bran replied, and his mother turned on him, shooing him toward the hall.

"You! Up to bed!"

"But—"

"You heard me! To bed! You saved Kathleen, now you go to sleep."

"With pleasure. Don't let her near me for the rest of my life."

They watched as Bran left the room, then Mrs. Vanelli turned to Kathleen with a wink.

"That's love talk. Boys always act like they don't want you when they want you *passionately."*

"Go home!" Bran yelled down.

"She stays!" his mother yelled back. "Go to bed!"

"Monica Franklin wants your phone number!" Kathleen couldn't resist. "She really misses you!"

"Miss him? Why does she miss him? That's that new girl—the blonde with all the hair!" Mrs. Vanelli wailed. "I don't want those bad girls calling here—that's why I keep the phone a secret."

"Ma, everyone knows the number!" Bran shouted.

"Then I'll change it!" she declared. "First thing tomorrow!"

For twelve years Mrs. Vanelli had been a widow —for twelve years she'd kept an unlisted phone number, even though Bran had always passed it around freely at school.

"So what about Monica?" Bran yelled back.

"She wants to sink her claws into you," Kathleen grumbled, then jumped as Bran suddenly appeared again in the doorway.

"In me?" He grinned. "Great!"

"Not great!" his mother threw back at him. "You're not going out with that girl!"

"Are you kidding?"

"Look at me—do I look like I'm making jokes?" Mrs. Vanelli puffed herself up with her most formidable scowl, and Bran promptly retreated. As Kathleen laughed, Bran's mother motioned her toward the table and started dishing up food from the stove.

"And what do you hear from your mother these days? Is she doing well?"

Kathleen sighed and settled herself into a chair. "She's got an apartment she really likes, and she's teaching English again. And she *still* wants me to come and live with her. Even though she *knows* we wouldn't get along. And even though I've told her a *million* times I'm not leaving my friends this last year of school. But you know Mom." Her face clouded, a mixture of anger and sadness. "She was always jealous of my friends."

Mrs. Vanelli shook her head and set a plate of

spaghetti down in front of Kathleen. "Because she *wanted* to be your friend, *cara*. She just never knew how. Your mother . . . she was always unhappy. Inside herself. Nothing to do with you."

"Yeah," Kathleen mumbled. "I guess." She looked up as Mrs. Vanelli sat across from her and reached over to pat her hand.

"I can't believe you're graduating this year. And what'll you do then? You away at school . . . Bran here for junior college . . ."

"I might *not* be going," Kathleen said. "With the alimony Dad's paying, I might end up staying right here."

"That's good. I don't want you to go. Bran doesn't want you to go."

"Bran doesn't think about me at all," Kathleen corrected with a smile. "Don't you ever get tired of playing matchmaker?"

"A mother can hope."

"He's a heartbreaker; you should know that by now. He could have any girl he wanted."

"He wants *you*. He just doesn't know it."

"He does not want me." Kathleen chuckled. "He's like my brother."

"Listen to me. Love starts with like."

"And anyway, Monica Franklin's after him. She's blond and gorgeous. They'd make a perfect couple."

"Perfect! He's got his father's nose, may Carlos rest in peace. With a nose that big, how can my son be perfect, I ask you?"

They both laughed. After a while Kathleen stabbed her fork into a mound of spaghetti and twirled it slowly, round and round.

"Try and eat," Mrs. Vanelli coaxed her. "You look worn out. I hope Bran didn't give you his flu."

"No, just trouble as always."

"That I believe." Mrs. Vanelli got up from the table, poured them both some coffee, and sat down again. "And how's our Della? I don't see much of her anymore."

"She's going out with some college guys," Kathleen said. "I don't see her much, either, outside of school, but we talk on the phone a lot. She's fine. Happy, I think."

"I like Della. She's a good girl." Mrs. Vanelli sighed and patted Kathleen's hand again. "You *need* good friends, *cara,* especially now. Eat your dinner. I want to make sure Bran took his pills."

Kathleen nodded. She waited till she heard Mrs. Vanelli climbing the stairs, then she walked over to the window and gazed out. It was still raining, and she felt more depressed than ever. The library books . . . the missing pictures and strange message . . . that feeling of being watched . . .

What's wrong with me? Maybe I'm more tired than I thought.

It embarrassed her now, thinking about the scene she'd made at the library. No wonder Bran had laughed at her. Here in the cozy warmth of the Vanelli kitchen, she wondered how she'd ever jumped to such ridiculous conclusions. No, Bran's idea made much more sense—that someone had used the books for some kind of school paper and helped themselves to the illustrations. He was right—Miss Finch *would* have a cow.

"He's asleep." Mrs. Vanelli's voice startled her, and she turned from the window. "You should go

43

look at him, Kathleen—he looks so sweet when he's sleeping."

Kathleen smiled and shook her head. "I'm going home. Dad should be there by now, and he'll wonder where I am."

"But the storm—and the dark—"

"Don't worry, I'll be fine. I'll cut between the houses and be home in five minutes."

"Just let me wake Bran—"

"No, let him sleep. He's already rescued me once tonight. I'll see you later, okay? And thanks for dinner."

"You didn't eat a bite," Mrs. Vanelli said, dumping the spaghetti into a container. "Here. Take it home. Have it for a bedtime snack."

Kathleen smiled. "Thanks." She hugged Mrs. Vanelli goodbye and opened the kitchen door. "And tell Bran I said thanks, too."

"He knows. But, yes, I'll tell him. And you tell that Monica I don't want her calling my son!"

Kathleen waved and closed the door behind her. Her own house was just four streets over, and it was an easy matter to slip through the side yards between the houses. She cut through the first block, then crossed the street. Lights glowed softly from windows; from time to time she could see people inside laughing . . . looking happy. It made her feel more alone than ever.

She cut through the next block and walked faster. Clouds hid the moon, and sporadic bursts of lightning flashed above the rooftops. Something rattled behind her, and she whirled to face it, a scream lodging silently in her throat. She could see now that it was just dead branches, tossed by the wind, but for just a moment it had sounded like footsteps. . . .

At last she came out directly across the street from her house. After hurrying up the walk, she let herself in, then slammed and locked the door behind her. *What's wrong with you anyway? One weird person decides to bring his books back to the library tonight, and you let it ruin your whole life.*

Annoyed with herself, Kathleen turned on the lights and made her way to the kitchen. Dad obviously wasn't home yet. She didn't feel like eating a bedtime snack—Mrs. Vanelli's spaghetti would have to wait. It wasn't even late—not quite ten o'clock—yet all she wanted to do was go to sleep.

She went upstairs to her room. She showered and got ready for bed, then lay there thinking about the library. No telling when Dad would be home—she remembered now, he had an important dinner tonight with clients and he'd told her not to wait up.

I might as well have stayed over at Bran's. Dad wouldn't have even noticed I was gone.

She didn't remember drifting off to sleep. . . .

She wasn't sure what woke her.

Tossing and turning, she drifted in a twilight state, back and forth through troubled dreams. The next thing she knew, she was on her back, staring up at the ceiling, and her throat felt raw, and tears were running down her face.

It must have been a nightmare . . . something painful and sad. . . .

Kathleen bolted upright.

Her eyes widened, and as she looked around at her bedroom, everything swam in a hazy gray light.

"Oh, God . . . oh God—"

Kathleen jumped out of bed. She started toward the door and saw long tendrils of smoke curling in beneath it.

"Dad!" she screamed. "Dad, wake up! There's a fire!"

She gasped and began to cough. Yanking her robe from the foot of her bed, she held it against her face.

She knew better than to try and open the door. Instead she ran to the window and flung it open. From up here she could see the empty driveway in front of the house, and as she realized her father's car wasn't there, a feeling of half relief-half panic surged through her. Frantically she began pushing at the screen.

"Help!" Kathleen screamed. "Somebody help me!"

She was dimly aware of the screen finally popping out . . . of it falling in slow motion, down, down into the yard below. A brief thought came to her to call 911, but in some distracted corner of consciousness she could already hear distant sirens. She swung herself to the windowsill and looked down in terror.

Someone was crouched at the edge of the lawn.

The shadow—the *human* shadow—pressed back into the trees where the streetlight couldn't reach, part of the night and the fog and the drizzling rain, and the blanket of smoke streaming over everything—

46

"You!" she screamed. *"Stop!"*

It ran. Like a ghost, it slipped completely away, losing itself among the other shadows of the night. One minute it was there watching her . . . the next minute it was as though the dark shape had never existed.

"Help!" Kathleen screamed again. "Please help me!"

Her throat was burning, constricting, cutting off her air. Her eyes felt like cinders, and she squinted, trying to focus beyond the grayness. Through the swirling smoke she was beginning to see movements—hear voices—neighbors calling and running, cars squealing along the street, flashing lights speeding toward the house.

She had no way of knowing how bad the fire was.

She only knew she had to get out.

She'd have to jump.

And she could see the firefighters now, waving their arms at her, shouting things, but her mind was going hazy like the smoke, and the voices seemed farther and farther away.

Slowly she put out one arm and tried to grab the drainpipe at the corner of the house. A firefighter yelled again; she stared at him like something in a dream.

She could feel the metal beneath her fingers . . . the rain upon her face. She'd been afraid to let go of the windowsill before, but now she was floating and everything would be all right. . . .

The sky cartwheeled above her.

Kathleen grabbed it and pulled the darkness down.

5

She's going to be fine," a voice said. "Just a little too much smoke. Wish I could say the same for your house, Tom."

Kathleen roused and looked around. She could hear people talking, but she couldn't see who or where they were. As her eyes swept slowly around the room, she knew it wasn't her own, and yet she also knew she belonged here.

"I hate to think what would have happened if she *hadn't* fainted," the voice went on. "I guess that firefighter was right there on his ladder trying to get ahold of her, but she kept fighting him."

More voices . . . more hushed conversation. Kathleen turned her head upon the pillow and moaned softly. Even without touching it, she could feel the huge knot on her head.

"She needs to rest." This time the voice got louder, sounded very firm. "She's had a hell of an experience. Let her sleep as long as she can."

Kathleen was wide awake now. She stared at the closed door of the room and felt tears fill her eyes. She knew that voice now—it was Dr. McNally, who'd taken care of her since she was born. She ran her hands along Mrs. Vanelli's homemade quilt and allowed herself one quiet sob.

"I just don't understand it." Her father's voice now, tired . . . numb. "How could it have happened? She's always so careful."

Kathleen frowned. She tried to sit up, but immediately sank back again. Her head felt heavy; it took all her strength to get out of bed. Putting her ear against the door, she listened for a moment, then let herself out into the hall. She perched near the top of the stairwell and looked down into the living room below, where a group of familiar faces had gathered.

"She's always careful," her father said again. "But I know *I* didn't leave the iron on. I haven't been down to the laundry room all week."

Kathleen frowned. *The iron? What's he talking about, the iron?*

"It doesn't matter," Mrs. Vanelli said firmly. "What matters is that Kathleen's all right. It could have been worse."

"She must have been so scared." Bran's voice now, sounding so serious. "Waking up all alone like that. We shouldn't have let her go home. Not to an empty house."

There was no mistaking the accusation in his tone. An uncomfortable silence dragged by until Mr. Davies finally spoke again.

"It looked a lot worse than it was," he said, almost defensively. "Smoke damage, for the most part. The fire was in the laundry room in the basement—it never spread upstairs—"

"She didn't know that," Bran said bluntly. "She tried to jump out the window so she wouldn't be burned alive."

"Bran," Mrs. Vanelli said quickly. "Why don't you go up and check on Kathleen—"

"No, Rosa, he's right to be angry with me," Mr. Davies said. "I should have been there. But I had this important meeting—and you never think something like this could happen to you." He thought a minute, then added, "I guess we'll just have to go to a motel till we get the place fumigated and—"

"You're not taking Kathleen," Mrs. Vanelli said firmly. This time there was no room for discussion in her tone, and Mr. Davies obviously knew better. "Kathleen stays with us. It will be better."

"She's right, Tom," Dr. McNally said, trying to be diplomatic. "At least for tonight. I've given Kathleen something to help her sleep—I'd rather she not be moved."

Mr. Davies considered this. Then "Yes," he said at last. "Yes, you're right. If you're sure we're not imposing—"

"Imposing!" Mrs. Vanelli burst out. "I love that child like my very own—and if you haven't figured that out by now, Tom Davies, you're a *bigger* fool than I've always thought you are. It's settled. She *stays*. And not just tonight. Till everything is back to normal."

Kathleen leaned against the wall with a wry smile. *In that case I'll be living here forever.*

"Then now's as good a time as any to bring this

up," her father said, looking somewhat sheepish. "Rosa, I'm supposed to go out of town on business tomorrow. I know it must seem like bad timing, but the truth is, it's been planned for months, and Kathleen's known about it. It's *crucial* that I go— other people are involved, and I can't change it or cancel it."

"Yes, yes, you go then." Mrs. Vanelli gave her disapproving frown. "Kathleen knows we want her. Her home is with us as long as she wants to stay."

Mr. Davies hesitated, then said meekly, "Yes. Yes, of course, that's so kind of you, Rosa. Thank you. As you know, things have been—"

"I know how things have been," Mrs. Vanelli cut him off. "This is better. For everyone. Just leave her tonight—Bran can get her things tomorrow."

"Will you tell her I said good night?" Mr. Davies asked.

"Yes. Don't wake her. Let her sleep."

Kathleen shut her eyes. There were footsteps . . . hushed good nights . . . the front door opening and closing. Mrs. Vanelli let loose with a string of Italian axioms, Bran jumping in here and there with a few choice expressions of his own. Opening her eyes again, Kathleen crept back to bed and had just laid down when the door inched open.

"You awake?" Bran whispered.

"Yes. Come in."

He left the door open. Soft light filtered in from the hallway, catching his silhouette as he glided across the room and eased down on the edge of her bed.

"How you feeling?" he asked.

Kathleen tried to smile "I'm not sure."

"It's okay. You should go back to sleep now."

"I don't think I can."

"Bet you'd be surprised."

She looked at him a moment, then sighed. "I heard you all talking down there. Guess you're stuck with me, huh?"

Bran grinned. "Who's stuck with who?"

"Good point."

"Yeah, *I* thought so."

"How bad's my house?"

"Not bad." His eyes flicked to the window. It was raining again, a soothing sound. "It's gonna smell for a while, though."

"I didn't start it," Kathleen said, and his eyes flicked back to her. "The iron. Dad said I left the iron on and started the fire. But I didn't use the iron today."

Bran looked back at her. "Go to sleep."

"I never touched that iron! And when I looked out my bedroom window, someone was running away."

Bran cocked his head. "Running away? From what?"

"I don't know. Me—the house—the fire."

"Was that before or after you passed out?"

"I didn't imagine it." Her voice rose tightly. "I wasn't dreaming, either. I *saw* someone, and he was watching me, and I think he started the fire."

Bran looked down at the quilt. "How?" he asked.

"I don't know."

"Kath—"

"He was running down the street! He hid in the trees, and then he ran away down the street!"

"Kath, listen to me." Bran leaned over and took one of her hands in his. "You know old Mr. Peterson next door to you?"

She nodded. Her throat felt full and sore.

"He was out jogging when he saw the smoke. He's the one who called the fire department."

Kathleen stared. It took several minutes for his words to sink in. At last she shook her head.

"This *wasn't* Mr. Peterson. This guy was hiding, and then he disappeared."

Bran nodded. "Okay," he said quietly. "Go to sleep."

"You don't believe me."

"Yeah, I believe you. We'll talk about it tomorrow."

Tears stung her eyes. She swallowed hard and put her arms across her face so he wouldn't see.

"You want anything?" Bran asked her.

She shook her head.

"I'm sorry, Kath," he whispered.

Behind him the door widened, light spilling in brighter from the hall. Mrs. Vanelli peered in, then motioned Bran to leave. She waited to hear his door slam, then came in and placed some things on the foot of the bed.

"Some dry things for you to wear, *cara*—a nightgown and robe and some slippers. Just for tonight. Tomorrow we'll get your own clothes."

She put one hand on Kathleen's forehead, leaning close with a tender smile.

"Get a good night's sleep. Sleep late in the morning. You know where we are if you need anything."

Kathleen nodded. Bran's room was right next door—his mother's was farther away, across the hall at the very end.

"Such a thing . . ." Mrs. Vanelli sighed, hugging Kathleen close, smoothing her hair. "A sad and terrible thing. But you're here with us now. You're safe."

"I know," Kathleen mumbled. "Thanks."

Mrs. Vanelli kissed her forehead and pulled away with a smile. "Sweet dreams."

Kathleen nodded. She watched as the door swung shut, leaving her alone. The lamp cast soft shadows across the old-fashioned furniture, the framed pictures of saints on the pale papered walls, the curtains at the window, drawn snugly against the night.

Kathleen reached for the nightgown. It was way too big for her, but it smelled nice and felt soft against her skin. She wrapped herself up in it like a cocoon and turned out the light, lying there in bed, staring drowsily up at the ceiling. *I did see someone running away . . . and it wasn't Mr. Peterson. . . .*

She was floating. She could see herself back in the library, and Alexander and Robin and Bran were all there with her, standing around and shaking their heads while she kept pointing at the book with the cutout pictures. . . .

HORRORS AWAIT YOU . . .

Kathleen's eyes flew open.

Dante's *Inferno.* Dante's journey through hell. And in hell there was, of course . . . fire.

54

6

You're not talking," Mrs. Vanelli fretted, pouring Kathleen some orange juice, pushing it across the table with a worried frown. "You're too quiet this morning."

"Yeah, it's nice," Bran mumbled into his toast.

His mother whacked him on the head with a dishtowel.

"Did you sleep okay, *cara?*" she fussed, shoveling eggs and bacon onto Kathleen's plate. "Were you warm enough?"

"I was fine." Kathleen forced a smile. "That bed's the most comfortable I've ever slept in."

"Something about that bed . . ." Mrs. Vanelli turned back to her skillet on the stove. "Everyone who sleeps in that bed says it's the best they've ever slept in. Even my son—even *he* says it's the best he's ever slept in. Like he's a connoisseur of beds!"

Kathleen turned and raised an eyebrow at Bran,

but he seemed to have suddenly discovered something intensely fascinating about his toast and wouldn't look at her.

"Do you have to work today? I wish you'd stay here," Mrs. Vanelli went on, buttering more bread, heaping it on top of Kathleen's bacon. Kathleen stared down at her plate in awe.

"Ma, look what you're doing." Bran sighed. "You're gonna make her sick."

"No, really, it's good," Kathleen said.

"I wish you hadn't gone back in your house," Mrs. Vanelli continued, passing Kathleen the jelly. "I'm sure it's not safe. I wish your father hadn't called you this morning."

"It's really okay," Kathleen assured her. "And I'm sort of glad to have it over with. Dad met me over there, and I got the stuff I needed, and he told me goodbye, and said he was sorry about the trip, but you know, it's something that can't be helped. And he was right about the house—the smoke was really the worst of it. Once the smell's gone, you won't be able to tell anything ever happened, unless you go down to the basement—"

She was babbling, and she knew it. She stopped abruptly, picked up her juice, and took a long swallow.

"That father of yours—" Mrs. Vanelli began, but Bran cleared his throat loudly and began pounding the ketchup bottle. Without warning, thick red liquid squirted out all over his plate and into his coffee cup. Bran stared down at it in dismay.

"Nice going," Kathleen said.

They all turned as the back door opened and a familiar voice greeted them.

"Morning, everyone!"

"Della!" Kathleen beamed at the sight of her friend. "Come on in!"

"Heard about the fire last night. Figured you'd be here." Della Conway slammed the door and shrugged out of her jacket. Music was blaring from her headphones, and as she slung them around her neck, she reached over to ruffle Bran's hair. He dodged her and kept on eating.

"Morning, Romeo." Della grinned. "How's it going?"

"Fine till you showed up," Bran said.

Della ignored him. She was as tall as Bran, probably even broader through the shoulders, amply endowed in every way, and incredibly feminine. She was the only one Kathleen knew who could wear pink hightops, crazy mismatched outfits, and a huge bow on her headphones, and still manage to carry it off in grand style.

"Breakfast!" Della eyed the table longingly. "Looks delicious!"

"Yeah, like you need it," Bran retorted.

This time both Della and Mrs. Vanelli hit him on the head. Bran winced and kept on chewing his toast.

"You sit down." Mrs. Vanelli gave Della a hug. "And you eat—look here, I've got plenty of food. I was just telling Kathleen yesterday how we don't get to see you anymore."

"Some of us really like that," Bran said.

Della shoved her chair up next to his and gave him a smug smile.

"Your wittiness is only rivaled by your brain. I think that pretty much says it all."

Bran shrugged and took a sip of coffee.

"He's so cute," Della purred, leaning over, squeezing Bran's cheek. "Isn't he just the cutest thing?"

"Monica Franklin thinks so," Kathleen couldn't help joining in. Bran pulled away from Della and tried to look indifferent, but Kathleen caught the quick flush over his cheeks.

"The dimple." She winked at Della. "I think it's the dimple that makes girls crazy."

"No . . ." Della tried to grab his chin, but Bran squirmed out of her grasp. "I think it's more . . . the eyes. Kind of reminds you of . . . I don't know . . . a basset hound?"

Bran stood up from the table. "I got things to do."

"They can wait," Mrs. Vanelli said. "You give Kathleen a ride to work. And take Della along."

"My car can't carry that much weight."

Della gave him a chilly smile. "I *won't* forget that."

"Elephants usually don't."

He ducked out the door as she aimed her purse at his head and let it fly. Kathleen smiled and went to the closet for her coat.

"I don't understand this." Mrs. Vanelli went after her. "Why you have to be working so much during spring break."

Kathleen looked almost apologetic. "Because I'm supposed to be in charge of things while Miss Finch is away at some seminar. Because—"

"Because you're gutless and you can't say no," Bran finished.

Kathleen scowled at him, then turned back to Mrs. Vanelli. "Please stop worrying about me."

"It's what I do, worry. I'm a mother." Mrs. Vanelli hugged her, then held her at arm's length. "I wish you'd stay here and rest—the doctor said you *need* to rest. It's shock you're feeling."

"But I did rest, and now I'm feeling just fine." Kathleen kissed her cheek, then followed Della outside. "I'll see you later. Oh, I almost forgot—I have to work till nine."

"I'll send Bran to pick you up," Mrs. Vanelli promised, going out with them onto the porch.

"What am I, a chauffeur?" Bran got into his car and slammed the door. "I got a date."

"With who?" his mother shouted.

Bran waved and started backing down the driveway. Kathleen and Della scrambled to get in the car.

"With who?" Mrs. Vanelli shouted louder. "Not one of those bad girls, you hear me—it better not be one of those girls!"

Bran revved the motor and took off down the street. Kathleen settled back and stared out the window; Della put her headphones on again and leaned forward from the back seat.

"Your mom's afraid Monica's going to corrupt you, Bran," Della teased.

Kathleen sighed. "If she only knew the truth . . ."

Bran slouched down behind the wheel. "She makes me crazy. Her . . . and you . . . and you. You *all* make me crazy."

"Hey—" Della turned her music low and put a

hand on Kathleen's shoulder. "Are you really okay? What happened last night?"

"An accident," Bran said quickly. "Someone left the iron on in the laundry room."

Della whistled. "My God, Kath, the whole place could've burned down."

"I know." Kathleen nodded glumly. "Let's not talk about it, okay?"

Della glanced at Bran in the rearview mirror. He gave an almost imperceptible shrug.

"Sure. Okay," Della agreed, forcing a smile. "We'll talk about whatever you want. Bran, what is *wrong* with this stupid car?"

Bran stared cooly at her reflection. "It's gasping for breath. It's not used to hauling two-ton freight around."

Della slid both hands around his neck. Slowly Bran's eyes widened.

"Now, be nice," Della said softly. "Or Monica Franklin will have to settle for a boyfriend with no head." She glanced at Kathleen, waiting for a follow-up insult, but Kathleen was staring at the floor, frowning.

"Remember last night?" Kathleen asked Bran.

Della looked suspicious. "Last night *what?*"

"Yes, I do," Bran choked, "and you were *great.*"

Kathleen frowned harder. Della shook Bran by the throat, then let him go.

"The library," Kathleen went on. "The bookmark with the writing."

"Yeah." Bran seemed to be thinking. "Yeah . . . Donny's Furnace, What about it?"

Kathleen gave him a withering look. "That's

Dante's *Inferno*. If anyone should know Italian, you should."

"I only know the dirty words." When she didn't laugh, he let out a sigh and tried to look solemn. "Okay, okay. What about it?"

"Don't you see? This book is all about what hell's supposed to be like. And then last night there's a fire in my house. Hell? Fire? Get it?"

She looked at Bran, and then at Della. Both of them stared back at her.

"I mean . . . he could have come in the basement window. No one probably thought to check because the fire just looked like an accident—but that window *never* locks tight. Anyone could get it open."

"Excuse me—" Della began, but Bran cut her off.

"Who could have gotten in your house? *Dante?"*

Kathleen glowered at him. "No. The guy running away."

"Mr. Peterson?"

"It wasn't Mr. Peterson. It was someone watching me."

"I've seen Mr. Peterson," Bran said reasonably. "And he watches every female on your street. Not that he'd know what to do with any of them."

"Bran—" Kathleen bristled, and he instantly looked contrite.

"Okay, you're right. I know this is serious."

"Will someone please tell me what's going on?" Della demanded.

Bran and Kathleen exchanged looks.

"Be my guest," Bran said.

As thoroughly as she could, Kathleen went over last night's events—from her first twinge of uneasiness in the library, to the damaged books and the strange message, to the fire and the figure she'd seen running from her yard. When she finished, Della reached over and gently patted her shoulder.

"So what you're saying is"—Della hesitated . . . took a deep breath . . . went on—"is that somebody tried to burn the house down with you in it."

"Great." Bran grimaced. "Thanks a lot, Del."

Kathleen closed her eyes. Several moments passed before she opened them again. "I hadn't thought about it that way," she mumbled. "But I guess so. Yes. With me in it."

"Well, shouldn't you tell the police or something?" Della worried.

"Come on, you're both ridiculous," Bran said, almost angrily. "Tell the police *what?* They'll laugh at you! Why would somebody do that, anyway, set a fire—they'd have to be crazy. It doesn't even make sense."

"I know it doesn't make sense," Kathleen mumbled. "But the library books don't make sense, either. And whoever I saw running away last night . . . *he* doesn't make sense, either."

Bran groaned. "We're back to that again."

"But as much as I hate to agree with Bran," Della said, tossing him a reluctant glance, "he does have a point. Kath, you don't have an enemy in the world."

"Well . . . at least not till now." Kathleen gave a dry laugh. "At least not that I ever knew about."

"And it really could have been something that innocent," Della went on reasonably. "Someone cutting out pictures to get a better grade on their paper. And just . . . you know . . . doodling around on a bookmark. I mean, stuff like that happens all the time."

"I know," Kathleen mumbled.

"And knowing how your dad is," Della went on, trading another glance with Bran, "I'd be willing to bet *he* left the iron on and doesn't even remember doing it. He's always been absentminded—all he ever thinks about is his work."

"I know," Kathleen said again.

She turned her head and stared out the window. It was an ugly part of town—buildings being razed and renovated, streets and sidewalks cluttered with Dumpsters and muddy equipment. The morning was gray and hazy, and the rain had slowed to a drizzle. Everything looked wet and weary and sad.

"So who's your date tonight, Bran?" Kathleen said with a sigh, ready to change the subject.

"Who are you, my mother?"

"You really *do* have a date?" Della looked incredulous. "Someone's actually that desperate?"

Bran didn't answer. As Della glanced over at him, she saw that his eyes were locked on the mirror, and he was frowning.

"What?" she teased. "No defense? You mean, you *agree* with me that some poor girl is actually so desperate—"

"Did you feel that?" Bran interrupted, and both Della and Kathleen turned in their seats.

"What?" Kathleen asked. "What are you talking about?"

"That," Bran mumbled. "Dammit—I think we got a flat."

63

While the girls looked on, he swung the car to the curb and got out. Walking around to the back, he stared down at the left rear tire, then hit his fist against the trunk.

"Look at this! Split wide open!"

Kathleen turned off the ignition. She and Della climbed out and joined him on the street.

"Is that normal?" Della asked, frowning at the gaping pieces of rubber.

"No, it's not normal. Someone's been screwing around with my car." Angrily Bran kicked the useless tire, then went back for his keys.

"You could have run over a nail or glass or something." Della tried to be helpful. "I mean, look at all the construction going on around here—this street's a mess!"

"We'll help," Kathleen said quickly. As Bran opened the trunk, she squeezed in and started rummaging around for tools. Bran found the spare and hauled it out, leaning it against the door.

"What are you doing?" Bran sighed. He could hear the faint beat of music coming from Della's headphones. As he stood back and watched, Della started swaying and singing to herself while she jacked up his car.

"What does it look like I'm doing?" she yelled at him. "What's the matter—does this offend your masculinity or something?"

"No, I just want you to be careful with my car."

"I've changed many a tire in my day, pal. And believe me, *nothing* could hurt this old wreck."

Bran grumbled under his breath and went back to the trunk. Kathleen was standing there with a strange look on her face, a small, square object held in her hands.

"What now?" he asked, coming up beside her. "You sick or something?"

"What's this doing here?" she asked quietly.

"Huh?" Looking over her shoulder, Bran stared down at the book. "What the hell's that?"

"Anna Karenina," Kathleen murmured. "Are you reading *Anna Karenina?"*

"Anne who? I've never even heard of her," Bran said. He grabbed it from her hands and frowned. "Geez, what next? Now I got someone leaving garbage in my car—"

"It's not garbage—it's a classic. By Tolstoy. About a woman who—"

The sound stopped her. It came from behind them and above, where the street rose to a sharp incline, and as she glanced quickly at Bran, she knew he'd heard it, too. She saw him turn around —the confusion on his face—the split-second realization as his cheeks drained white—

"Oh, Jesus," he whispered.

It was heading straight for them.

The huge truck veering across the road—rapidly gaining speed as it barreled down the hill—

"My God," Kathleen mumbled, "there's nobody driving—"

Bran shoved her. He shoved her hard toward the curb, and yelled at her to run. Kathleen stumbled, and as she fell, she saw Della in her headphones, dancing backward into the street—

"Della!" she screamed.

But Della didn't hear.

She was singing to herself and smiling, and as Kathleen froze in horror, Bran flung himself into the road.

"No!" she shrieked.

But she couldn't see them anymore—

Only the huge wheels roaring past her as the truck swerved sideways and crashed on the other side of the street.

ella!" Kathleen screamed. *"Bran!"*

She couldn't move.

She was screaming and crying, but her legs wouldn't work, wouldn't lift her up, wouldn't carry her off the curb—

She heard people shouting.

She saw people running from buildings.

And then at last she was running, too, shoving people aside as she fought to get near the wrecked truck.

"Someone call an ambulance!" a man yelled.

A woman gasped and started to cry.

"No . . ." Kathleen whispered. "God . . . no . . ."

Della was covered with blood. Her body lay twisted at a macabre angle, legs bent beneath her, arms splayed out at her sides. Her headset was gone. Her brown hair was wet and red.

Kathleen couldn't see Bran.

She couldn't find him anywhere.

"Bran!" she screamed again. "Oh, Della—"

"Get back!" Someone tried to hold her, but she fought her way through.

"Let go of me! They're my friends!"

And arms were pulling her—trying to restrain her—and from somewhere in the distance she heard a different voice call out, "Here's another one!"

She struggled free and ran.

He was lying facedown on a patch of grass. She could hear him moaning, and her heart leaped into her throat.

"He's alive," someone said. "What about the girl?"

Kathleen crumpled to her knees. She wanted to touch him—to hold him—but she couldn't. She didn't want to see what he looked like. She was afraid.

"Della," Bran mumbled.

He rolled over. He moaned and lay there on his back and stared up at Kathleen without recognizing her. Blood ran from his nose and mouth and gushed from his chin. His clothes were splattered with it. His face was chalk white.

"Bran," Kathleen whispered. She took his hand . . . squeezed it . . . felt it go limp. "Bran, can you hear me? You're going to be okay."

But he didn't hear her. She was half aware of the paramedics pushing their way through, and she was babbling, trying to get someone to listen to her. A policeman started asking her questions, but she just kept shaking her head.

"It rolled down the hill—there wasn't anybody

driving—he tried to save us—" The policeman was nodding, writing in a notebook, staring at her. "My friends"—Kathleen squeezed his arm—"are they okay?"

Nobody would answer. Kathleen stood numbly while the ambulance took Bran and Della away. She felt the policeman take her arm and steer her toward his car . . . heard him say they would take her to the hospital.

"Yes," she mumbled to him. "Yes, yes . . . I just want to get Della's things."

She went to Bran's car.

She found her own purse, and then she found Della's in the backseat.

She walked around to the trunk.

She was staring and she could feel her lips moving, but no words were coming out—they were all in her head, going round and round and round. . . .

Anna Karenina . . . I remember what happened. . . . She threw herself in front of a train. . . .

Kathleen leaned into the trunk.

She reached for the book, but it wasn't there.

8

"How long has it been now?" Mrs. Vanelli whispered. She sat on the edge of her chair, rosary beads dangling from her fingers. Even in anguish, her face was still strong, yet Kathleen could hardly bear to look at it. Instead she stared at the clock on the waiting room wall and watched the slow, ponderous movement of the hands.

"I wish he was at the clinic," Mrs. Vanelli fretted. "I wish he was at the clinic and not here at the hospital. I hate hospitals!"

Kathleen reached over and patted her hand. "Our little clinic's not set up to deal with things like this, you know that. Brookside Hospital's a nice hospital. And anyway, Dr. McNally's still taking care of him."

"Why did this happen?" Mrs. Vanelli asked softly. "Why, to these dear children? You never expect something like this—it's just not normal. . . ."

And no, Kathleen wanted to shout, *it's not normal, it's freaky, and it's all wrong, and why won't anyone believe me . . . ?*

She hadn't said anything to the police—how would it have sounded? *There was this book in the trunk of our car, but no, it's not there anymore, and anyway, I'm afraid it was a warning right before my friends got run down by a truck. . . .*

Kathleen covered her face with her hands. Maybe the book hadn't been real after all. Maybe she'd just imagined it. . . .

But Bran saw it, too.

She'd wait and talk to Bran before she said anything. Bran would know what to do.

"Rosa?"

Dr. McNally came into the room, his face kind but soberly professional. He was still in his scrubs, and both Kathleen and Mrs. Vanelli braced themselves.

"Yes." Mrs. Vanelli took Kathleen's arm, her voice surprisingly steady. "Yes, tell me."

"He's going to be fine," the doctor said slowly. "He's got some bad cuts and bruises—a broken wrist. I had to stitch up his chin. But he'll be fine."

"And Della?" Kathleen whispered.

His face remained carefully composed. "I've just spoken with her parents. She's still in a coma. We can't tell much at this point. Brain damage . . . paralysis . . . there's no way of knowing. She had severe internal injuries. She's a very sick girl."

Kathleen's eyes filled with tears. She felt Mrs. Vanelli squeeze her hand.

"She *will* come through this," Mrs. Vanelli said

firmly. "She will. And be our Della again." She took a deep breath. "When can I see my son?"

Dr. McNally gave a weary smile. "They're taking him up to his room now, but he's not awake. And I think I'd better warn you, when he does wake up, there's a chance he might not remember anything that happened. It's very common . . . nothing to worry about. He might remember it someday . . . or he might not."

Mrs. Vanelli reached out and took the doctor's hand. "Thank you. Thank you for saving my boy."

Kathleen went slowly up the sidewalk to the library.

She turned and waved goodbye to Mrs. Vanelli, then watched as the car disappeared down the street. She'd wanted Bran's mother to go home and rest for a while, but she knew Mrs. Vanelli would only take time to change clothes, make a few phone calls, then head straight back to be with Bran. The hospital was a half hour's drive away. Fremont Clinic was well equipped for handling minor emergencies, but serious cases always went to Brookside.

Kathleen turned back again with a sigh. Her feet felt like lead weights, and as she reached the porch, she noticed the front door was slightly ajar.

I wasn't here on time, and the library was unlocked all night, and Robin's probably wondering where I am, and Miss Finch'll be furious. . . .

She wasn't too worried about people who might have come in already—she knew Robin could check books out if he absolutely had to. He'd certainly watched her do it enough times, and she'd even coached him when Miss Finch wasn't looking.

Still, she glanced down at her watch now and groaned. Nearly four o'clock. *With any luck, someone stole all the books last night, and I'll get fired and never have to work in this stupid place again . . .*

To her surprise the main room was empty. Robin was on a ladder, straining his arms toward a light fixture in the ceiling, and he glanced down at her with a worried frown.

"Robin, I'm so sorry—yes, I'm fine, I'm fine," Kathleen assured him. "Is anyone here?"

He nodded and held up a finger.

"Where?"

Robin motioned toward the staircase as Kathleen pulled off her coat.

"Upstairs. What time did you get here?"

Ten fingers went up.

"Well, at least one of us is responsible." Kathleen sighed. "Was Miss Finch absolutely fuming? You can tell me—I can take it."

Robin grinned. He climbed to the very top of the ladder and stretched again, his lean body perfectly balanced in midair. While Kathleen watched nervously, he placed the bulb in the socket and carefully screwed it in. His hands worked quickly, and as he tilted his head back, his long dark hair swished back and forth across his shoulderblades.

"Robin, you're scaring me—please be careful."

The dark eyes looked down at her. In one graceful movement Robin lowered his arms and descended the ladder, coming to stand beside her with an apologetic smile.

"So do I still have a job?" Kathleen asked.

He moved to the desk, picked up a notepad and pencil, and wrote, handing it over to her.

SHE DIDN'T COME.

"What?" Kathleen stared at him. "You mean, after that big lecture yesterday, she took off for her stupid seminar and forgot to leave the keys?"

He shrugged . . . nodded.

"Yes, I guess so, too," Kathleen murmured. It wasn't like Miss Finch to forget. A sudden chill went through her, and she forced it away. "The front door didn't shut last night, Robin. I came back for my purse, and the door was unlocked. So now what are we going to do about closing up at night?"

He took hold of her shoulders and shook his head. Then he motioned her to follow him and headed for the kitchen. As Kathleen watched, mystified, he pried up a piece of linoleum, stuck his hand beneath the floor, and pulled out a bunch of keys.

"What's that?" Kathleen stared at him. "You don't mean these are extras?"

Robin nodded.

"But how—where—"

He took the notepad back and scribbled.

I HAD THEM MADE.

"*You* did?" In spite of her weariness, Kathleen had to smile. "Let me guess. In case she ever lost hers. Because she only has the one set." She shook her head and added, "So I guess you stole the originals out of her desk drawer."

Robin nodded. Kathleen went over to him and took the keys, then tilted her head against his chest.

"Robin"—she sighed—"what would I ever do without you?"

He stood there, not moving, arms at his sides.

Kathleen felt the soft flannel of his shirt beneath her cheek . . . the faint rise and fall of his breathing. She took a deep breath and choked back tears.

"Robin, something terrible's happened. Bran and Della were in an accident, and they're both in the hospital. That's why I'm so late—it happened this morning and——"

"Oh," said a voice from the doorway. "Sorry."

Kathleen whirled around. Alexander was standing there looking in at them, and Robin immediately backed away.

"What are you doing?" Kathleen demanded.

"Trying to find . . . biographies," he said. He glanced quickly around the kitchen and added, "Wait—let me guess. The cookbook section?"

Kathleen ignored his attempt at humor and drew a shaky breath. "Biographies are upstairs. Last room on the left."

"Upstairs. I missed that one. Thanks a . . ." His voice trailed away, and he frowned, eyes narrowing behind his glasses. "Are you all right?"

"Yes. I'm fine." Lifting her chin, she tried to compose herself. "Like I said, biographies are upstairs."

"Upstairs," he said again, this time with a knowing look. "And we'd very much like to be alone now, Alexander, thank you very much."

He turned to leave, but Kathleen's voice stopped him.

"Wait. I'm sorry—you're wrong about what you're thinking—you're not interrupting anything. . . ." She turned to Robin, but he'd already slipped out the back door. Frustrated, she faced Alexander again and burst out, "I was just telling him, my two best friends are in the hospital."

"What?" Alexander looked shocked. He hesitated, then came slowly into the room. "What happened?"

"My friends Bran and Della . . . they got hit by a truck. They . . ." She looked at the floor and felt a tear trickle down her cheek. *Don't cry—don't cry—you won't be able to stop—*

A hand touched her shoulder. She glanced up into Alexander's face and saw his look of concern.

"Bran?" he mumbled. "The guy I met last night?"

Kathleen nodded. Suddenly she felt cold; it was all she could do to keep from shivering.

"Well . . . are they okay?" Groping for a kitchen chair, Alexander pulled it over and gently sat her down.

"Bran is—or will be—but they don't know about Della yet." Kathleen swallowed hard. "The whole thing was so freaky, I . . ."

"How did it happen?"

He was leaning over her now, but as a muffled sound came from the porch, Alexander's head came up sharply. Glancing at the door, Kathleen could see just the faintest outline of a shadow through the screen, and she put a restraining hand on his arm.

"It's okay, it's just Robin."

"Does he always lurk around like that?"

"He's not lurking," Kathleen said, almost angrily. "We were having a conversation until you came in and ran him off."

"*I* ran him off?" Alexander sounded surprised.

"I didn't mean to run anyone off. Tell him to come back in."

Kathleen shook her head. "It wouldn't do any good," she insisted, lowering her voice. "He's not comfortable around people, and he doesn't talk. Not because he wouldn't like to, but because he can't. He's mute."

Alexander pondered this a moment. "I thought you said you were having a conversation."

"We were. We always do."

He hesitated once more, a faintly amused smile playing at the corners of his mouth. "So he's out there keeping an eye on you, is that how it is?"

"How what is?" Kathleen mumbled. She didn't even know why she was sitting here. She didn't want to be with Alexander, didn't want to talk about the accident—didn't even want to think about it. Every time she shut her eyes, she could still see Della backing into the street and Bran flinging himself in front of the truck. . . .

"So," Alexander said quietly. He pulled up another chair and sat down. "Do you want to talk about it?"

She shook her head no, but in that same split second the whole scene played itself out again in her mind. *No . . . no . . .* She rubbed her forehead, trying to push the images away, hearing herself even though she was trying not to remember. "I was on my way here this morning. . . . Bran was driving me, and Della was with us. We had a flat . . . and then we got out, and then this truck . . ." She stopped . . . shut her eyes . . . opened them again. "This truck came out of nowhere. It didn't have a driver, and it was out of control. Bran tried to push Della out of the way and . . ."

She couldn't go on. It took her several minutes to even realize that Alexander had ahold of her shoulders and was peering hard into her face.

"Don't," he murmured. "Just . . . try not to think about it anymore."

Try not to think about it. Like trying not to breathe. . . .

"It could have been worse," he said softly. "You could have been hurt, too."

Kathleen stared at him. She stared at him, and she felt a slow, cold anger go through her.

"That's right," she murmured. "They were hurt, and I wasn't. That certainly makes me feel wonderful."

"I didn't mean—"

"Forget it, I have to go to work," Kathleen said stiffly, getting up, moving past him to the hall. "I don't have time to stand around talking—I've got too much to do."

"Kathleen—"

"Oh, yes . . . biographies, right? Next time you come out of the Fremont Collection, take a left instead. The last door at the end of the hall. You can't miss it."

She didn't wait for him to answer. She hurried off through the maze of connecting chambers until she reached the main room of the library. Everything still looked deserted—no sign of anyone browsing today—and Kathleen continued on, past the front desk, then through a doorway that led to the other half of the first floor.

This west wing was the oldest part of the library.

For years Miss Finch had struggled to keep it in some semblance of repair, but Fremont just didn't have the funds to maintain such an old monstrosity. Two weeks ago the board had turned down a request for a new children's room—something bright and cheerful and inviting to encourage kids to read—so Miss Finch had decided to tackle the project herself. That's where Robin came in. Robin who could do almost anything with his hands and who loved solitary work. Now, as Kathleen stopped to catch her breath, she leaned in through the door and surveyed the general mess.

The room was dark and gloomy, hideously stained with mildew and waterspots, festooned with cobwebs, its windows caked with grime. Dampness and rot had taken their toll on everything—floorboards, paneling, mirrors, and shelves—and ragged wallpaper hung in brittle strips around what was left of a massive marble fireplace.

Poor old room . . . it looks just like I feel.

Shivering, Kathleen stepped across the threshold and moved slowly toward the middle of the floor. It was so cold in here—piercingly cold—and as she rubbed goose bumps from her arms, her eyes automatically swept over the tall windows on the opposite wall. She could see now that several panes of glass were broken near the sill, and as she made a mental note to tell Robin, she walked over to inspect the damage.

It was hard to see anything from these windows. Not only were they protected by thick metal bars, but on this particular end of the building, shrubs and evergreens pressed right up against them, so the view was one of leaves and branches and not much else. Kathleen leaned down and studied the pane, frowning at the jagged shards of glass that rose up, still intact, and the slivers that had sprayed across the floor. When had it happened? she wondered. She closed her eyes and tried to think. She knew she'd been in here early yesterday evening, helping Robin move some tools—she was sure they would have noticed the window if it had been broken then. . . .

She bent lower, studying the glass. Vandalism? It'd be impossible to throw something from a moving car or even the sidewalk and get it through all the bars and foliage. Which meant whoever did it had to have been right outside the window trying to reach in.

Trying to break in?

Kathleen gave a deep shudder. Had it happened last night when she was alone in the library? Or after she'd gone home? Whoever it was would have no way of knowing, of course, that the front door was unlocked all night . . . *or maybe they did know, maybe they just didn't want to take a chance on being seen.* . . .

Slowly Kathleen stretched out her arm.

She put her hand out through the hole and through the bars, fingers dangling in the cold, cold air.

Yes . . . if someone was standing right outside the window, they could stick something between the bars and break the glass—and with the windowsill so rotten, they might be able to work the bars free. . . .

She started to pull her hand back in.

OVERDUE

She didn't see the sudden movement in the bushes—didn't see the thing clamp down around her wrist—

She only knew that something had ahold of her, something strong and forceful, and that her arm was twisting sideways as she felt herself being slammed against the window—

A ragged, searing pain shot through her. Her hand and arm raked across the broken glass.

And then she was being shoved—backward and off balance—and as she fell to the floor, Kathleen finally was able to scream.

She lay there on the floor, too stunned to move.

She lay there and listened for someone to come, but when minutes crawled by and there was no sound of footsteps, she pulled herself into a sitting position and looked at the window.

Empty.

Only the broken panes of glass near the sill, just as they'd been when she'd first come into the room.

But not everything was the same. . . .

And as reality began to sink in, she was aware of an agonizing pain on her right side, and she looked down to see her arm and hand covered in blood.

"Oh, my God . . ."

Shakily she got to her feet. She stumbled to the door and shouted for Robin, and then she slowly made her way back toward the main room of the library, holding the walls for support. She felt sick at her stomach. She couldn't believe what had happened.

"Robin!" she shouted again. "Where are you?"

She started into the front room, then stopped abruptly and pulled back into the shadows of the hall. While she'd been gone, several people had come in, and she could see them now, wandering among the bookshelves, reading at tables, browsing through the card catalog. She leaned her head back against the wall and took a deep breath.

Oh, Robin, where are you . . . ?

She wasn't sure she could stay on her feet, and she didn't want to walk out there and faint in front of everyone. She was weak-kneed and dizzy. Looking down, she noticed thick red drops splattering on the floor around her foot.

Oh, Robin, please come. . . .

Then, to her surprise, she saw Alexander.

He was walking in through the front door of the library, and as he closed the door quietly behind him, he glanced anxiously toward the main desk. A few people were milling about, waiting to check out books, looking for someone to help them.

Kathleen grimaced against a wave of pain. She'd assumed Alexander was upstairs with the biographies—so what was he doing outside?

She watched as he ran one hand back through his windblown hair. He took off his glasses and rubbed them distractedly on his shirttail.

Kathleen crept as far over the threshold as she dared. She gritted her teeth, gestured with her good arm, and tried to call softly.

"Alexander!"

At first she thought he hadn't heard. He started across the floor, but then as she gestured again, she saw him hesitate . . . glance around . . . finally turn in her direction.

"Alexander—over here!" she hissed.

His eyes narrowed. She saw his mouth open— the quick glance he threw around the room. She put her finger to her lips, warning him to be quiet. He nodded, then walked nonchalantly toward her hiding place.

He reached her just in time. As she swayed, he caught her with both arms and firmly held her up.

"Going somewhere? Not a good idea," he mumbled, frowning down at her injuries.

"Can you please find Robin?"

"Forget Robin—I'm taking you to the doctor. What *happened?*"

"Someone—" She looked at him helplessly, knowing how unbelievable it was going to sound. "Someone was trying to break in—he tried to pull me through the window."

Alexander nodded slowly. "Let me get this straight. They wanted to come *in*—so they tried to pull you *out.*"

"I—he grabbed my hand and pulled me through the broken glass."

Alexander stared. "You actually saw someone."

"Well . . . not exactly—"

"You actually saw someone at the window, trying to pull you through."

"Well . . ." She stopped, her mind whirling in confusion. "No . . . that is . . . I *felt* something—a hand. I mean, it all happened so fast—"

"All right, don't try to talk."

"You've got to find Robin—*please!*"

He nodded his head, lowering her gently to the

floor, then yanked off his jacket and wrapped it tightly around her arm. "Wait here. And hold that."

She watched as he walked off. She closed her eyes and bit her lip, trying not to cry. The pain was horrible now—her whole arm was throbbing. She didn't know how long Alexander was gone—the next thing she knew, Robin was on his knees beside her, and Alexander was behind him, leaning over and frowning.

"Robin's going to take you, understand?"

"But—how—"

"He's using my car. Don't worry, I've worked in libraries before—I'll manage things here till you get back. Keep that around her arm," he told Robin. "Just get her there fast."

Robin nodded. The two of them got her on her feet again, and Alexander went directly to the main desk. They could hear him chatting with people and laughing as he started checking out their books. Robin put his arm around Kathleen, then guided her quickly through the room and out the front door.

"Can you drive?" Kathleen asked him as they hurried along the sidewalk. "I didn't know you could drive."

In spite of the situation Robin looked almost amused. He herded her toward a car parked at the curb and helped her inside.

The clinic wasn't far. As Robin maneuvered swiftly through back streets, Kathleen wound the jacket tighter and leaned back against the seat, closing her eyes.

Alexander doesn't believe me.

She tried to think back—back to when she was standing at the window. She could remember putting her hand through the hole . . . the rush of chilly air from outside . . . then that sudden, panicky feeling of fingers closing around her wrist. . . .

But he's right . . . I didn't really see it . . . I didn't really see anything. . . .

She glanced over and saw Robin watching her. His eyes flicked back to the road, and he reached over, covering her hand with his own.

"Did Alexander tell you what happened?" Kathleen asked tiredly. She waited for Robin to give some sign, but he kept his gaze straight ahead. "Someone was outside the window . . . I think he might have been trying to break in. You know . . . in the children's room. He must have heard me. He grabbed my arm and pulled . . ."

Her voice trailed off as Robin glanced at her. His brows drew together in a worried frown.

"It's true," Kathleen insisted. "I felt a hand on my arm, and I couldn't get away. Robin, something really weird's going on that I don't understand."

She straightened and turned toward him, her voice urgent.

"Listen—you remember what I told you about Bran and Della and the accident? Well, there's something else. There was a fire at my house last night. And I saw someone running away."

Robin threw her a look of alarm. He pulled his hand back and clamped it hard onto the steering wheel.

"It's okay—the fire, I mean, there wasn't much damage," Kathleen went on wearily. "The firemen said somebody left the iron on in our laundry room—except I *know* nobody used it yesterday. So now I'm staying at Bran's house. At least till my dad gets back from his stupid business trip."

Again Robin threw her a glance. Kathleen leaned toward him and frowned.

"I could have been killed last night. And Bran could have been killed this morning. And Della . . ." She bit her lip and put a hand to her mouth. "If Della dies, I don't know what I'll do."

Robin swerved around a corner. Kathleen winced and pressed the jacket tight against her arm.

"You didn't see the two of them like I did. And afterward—I went with Mrs. Vanelli to Bran's room. He wasn't awake yet, and he was all swollen and bruised and had these bandages—I couldn't stand to see him like that. And they wouldn't let me see Della at all. Her parents are so scared. . . ."

She drifted off, remembering. Then she drew a deep breath and put her hand on Robin's shoulder.

"Don't you see?" Kathleen said miserably. "The fire . . . the broken window . . . and I was *with* Bran and Della this morning! *They* got hurt, but *I* was with them! Robin . . . what if someone's after me, and I don't know why!"

His dark eyes widened. A look of bewilderment crossed his face, and he slowly shook his head.

"Just listen to me," Kathleen insisted. "Remember how I told you I went back to the library last night to get my purse? Well, that's when it started. While I was there, something happened—"

She went over everything—the book titles, the mutilated pages, the bookmark with the ominous message. She told him about the fire at her house . . . the details of the accident that morning . . .

finding the book in Bran's trunk . . . and how the book had vanished when she went back.

"But I know I didn't imagine that," she told Robin. "Bran saw the book, too. He was standing right there with me."

They had reached the clinic now. As Kathleen pulled away and shifted the jacket around her arm, Robin parked the car in front of the building.

"The *Inferno,*" Kathleen mumbled. "Fire. And *Anna Karenina* . . . only a truck instead of train."

For a long moment there was silence. Robin stared at the dashboard, his expression troubled.

"Don't you see?" Kathleen went on, pulling at his sleeve. "It's like these books are . . . I don't know . . . warnings. Premonitions. Not really literal, exactly—but more like some kind of sick game. It just doesn't make sense."

She couldn't tell what he was thinking. He helped her into the clinic and handed her over to the nurse. Judy had been working there ever since Kathleen could remember, and she made Kathleen comfortable in one of the examination rooms.

"What'd you do to yourself?" Judy fussed, getting her ready for the doctor. "Not a very good start to spring break."

Kathleen gave her a wry smile. "Just lucky, I guess."

"I'll say. Doc'll be in, in a minute."

"Won't he be surprised," Kathleen muttered.

If she hadn't been in such pain, it would have been almost comical, seeing the look on Dr. McNally's face. Having just seen her that morning, he was shocked to see her again so soon. Kathleen made some excuse about helping Robin repair the new room at the library, and how she'd slipped on some broken glass.

She rode back with Robin in silence. She'd needed stitches, and her arm and hand ached beneath their bandages. As the two of them walked into the library again, she was glad to see that most of the people had cleared out. Alexander was sitting behind the desk reading, and he looked up expectantly when he saw them.

"Not fatal, I hope," he said.

Kathleen shook her head and handed him back his jacket. "No. But I owe you a new jacket."

"Forget it. Just say it was sacrificed to a worthy cause."

"Did they beat the doors down while I was gone?"

"Not bad." He stood up, put a hand on her elbow, and steered her toward the hall. "Come on. I think I know what happened."

Reluctantly she went with him to the children's room. While Robin waited in the doorway, Alexander led Kathleen over to the window and pointed at the floor.

"Look," he said. "No wonder you fell through the glass. I almost did myself."

Kathleen followed the direction of his finger.

She saw the floorboards beneath the window, and the way they'd rotted through, leaving a gaping hole.

A hole that hadn't been there before.

10

o," Kathleen said slowly.

She turned around, looking first at Robin, then at Alexander. Both boys were staring at her, both of them looking decidedly uncomfortable.

"No," Kathleen said again, more adamantly this time. "No, that hole wasn't there when I was in here before."

The silence stretched out. Alexander shifted slightly and crossed his arms over his chest.

"I think what happened was . . . you must have stepped here, and it threw you off balance."

"But I'm trying to tell you, the hole wasn't there," Kathleen insisted.

Alexander nodded, his tone patient. "But it wouldn't have been there, would it. Because it didn't break through till you stepped on it."

Kathleen had started to deny it, but now the argument died in her throat. She stared at the floor and saw the obvious signs of rot and damp . . . frantically she tried to remember each detail of what had happened. *I leaned over to put my hand through the hole . . . so I must have taken a step . . .*

"I felt something," she mumbled. "Around my wrist."

"You said it happened so fast," Alexander reminded her, and Kathleen nodded and covered her face with her hands.

"I don't know," she admitted wearily. "I'm not sure."

"Why don't you go on home. Get some rest."

"I can't. We're open late tonight."

"I'll stay," he volunteered. "I can study just as easy at the front desk as upstairs."

From the doorway Robin nodded. Kathleen gave a wan smile.

"Thanks—I really appreciate it. But Miss Finch would have a fit. She's already going to be upset when people tell her some stranger was working here today." She sighed and examined her bandages. "At least I can show her my scars to prove I had a good excuse."

She moved past Robin into the hall. She went out to the desk and eased herself into the chair behind it.

Alexander frowned. "Are you sure you feel okay?"

Kathleen nodded and dug into the pocket of her jeans. "He gave me some pain pills. They should get me through till nine." She put the bottle on the counter and frowned at it.

"Why don't you just close up?" Alexander

coaxed. "Are the people in Fremont going to die if the library closes early one time?"

"No, but Miss Finch will." Kathleen glanced at the clock and waved them both away. "I'm fine. Go find something to do, both of you."

She saw the looks they exchanged before they went their separate ways—Alexander back to his research upstairs, and Robin off to the kitchen. Kathleen sighed and settled down, trying to ignore the pain in her arm. She opened the drawer and began to go over the list Miss Finch had left, but she couldn't concentrate. The unsettling events of the day kept playing over and over in her mind—she put the list down and covered her face with her hands.

Even Robin doesn't believe me. . . . They both think I'm crazy.

She tried to recall everything that had happened since last night, telling herself all of it could be explained . . . that she was making mountains out of molehills . . . that her imagination was working overtime. *Kids playing pranks . . . the iron left on . . . a runaway truck . . . an old floor rotting through . . .*

But the book in the trunk . . . Even Bran hadn't recognized it, hadn't known what it was doing there—but he could back up her story, because he'd seen it. And if she could only show those other library books to Robin—the ones from the bookdrop last night—then maybe he'd take her more seriously.

Kathleen pulled her chair closer to the desk and frowned. She distinctly remembered leaving those books on the desk last night when Bran had come for her—but where were they now? She searched through the piles of clutter, but they weren't anywhere on the counter, nor were they behind the desk in any of the cubbyholes or on any of the shelves.

Kathleen tried to think. Robin had been here all morning, but though he sometimes helped by checking out books, he never reshelved them. Alexander had been here a short while, of course—but he'd been studying, and she couldn't imagine he'd taken time to put any books away.

Puzzled, Kathleen checked the files and found the location of each title. Then she went directly into the next room and began hunting for the books on tortures and executions.

They weren't there.

A thorough search showed that the books weren't on the shelves where they were supposed to be. Kathleen looked around on the tables, but found nothing. Going back to the files, she made sure nobody had checked them out today. Again she pored through the shelves, thinking maybe someone had accidentally put them back in the wrong place, but she turned up nothing.

With growing uneasiness, Kathleen zeroed in on the classics. *Anna Karenina* wasn't on its shelf, either, and as she quickly scanned the rows of titles, she saw at a glance that the top shelf where *Inferno* should be had an empty space with no book in it.

Kathleen tried to reach the shelf, but it was just too tall. Hunting along the aisles, she finally found a stepstool and dragged it over, climbing up and trailing her forefinger along the numbers on the spines of the books.

Yes, this was the shelf, all right. But the book was missing.

Maybe someone pushed it back where I can't see. . . .

She stretched her left arm as far as she could, easing her hand up onto the shelf. Groaning softly, she stretched more, her fingers curling over the edge, groping back into the dark, narrow space.

And then she felt something . . . but it wasn't a book.

It was rounded and feathery, and very stiff, and as Kathleen recoiled in horror, her fingers knocked it off the shelf.

She felt it hit her shoulder, and she screamed and tried to brush it off. Dodging sideways, she slid off the stool and sprawled, crying out again as her wounded arm made contact with the floor. The thing landed beside her—right next to her face— so she could see every grisly detail.

The bird had been dead for some time.

It was stiff and cold and its wings were clotted with dark, dried blood.

A pencil was rammed through its heart.

And on its red breast, impaled there by the pencil, was a ragged piece of paper—a section of page torn from a book—

Come hither, sweet robin, and be not afraid,
    I would not hurt even a feather.

11

Her screams echoed through the high ceilings of the library. Before she even knew what was happening, Robin was there, pulling her to her feet, and kicking the horrible thing away.

"Oh, God . . ." Kathleen said brokenly. "Oh, Robin . . ."

He steered her to a chair, then went over to the thing in the corner. Lifting it gingerly by one end of the pencil, he held it up and silently read the message. As he lowered the dead bird, Alexander rounded the corner of an aisle and stopped in his tracks.

"Now what?"

"Now will you believe me?" Kathleen whispered.

"Believe you about what? What's going on?"

She tried to point, her arm shaking furiously. "It's a warning. It's a warning for Robin—"

"A warning?" Alexander covered the last few feet and took the dead bird from Robin. He scanned the message quickly, then made a face and held the thing at arm's length. Robin promptly took it and left the room.

"It's a message," Kathleen whispered. "A warning."

Alexander was watching her closely. At last he said, "And how do you figure that?"

"You read it, didn't you?" she said, her voice rising. "You saw what it said!"

Alexander nodded slowly. "Yes, but what—"

"It's an old nursery rhyme! Don't you see? Someone's going to hurt Robin! It's a warning! He's in *danger!*"

"Kathleen"—Alexander's smile was tentative—"it's just a joke. A sick one, granted, but nothing more than that."

She stared at him. She heard a slight movement behind her and turned to see Robin in the doorway.

"It was up on the shelf," she turned to Robin, trying to make him understand. "Up there where *Inferno* should have been—only it's not there now and nobody checked it out! Someone must have known I'd be looking for it—someone took it again and put that bird in its place—on purpose!"

"What's she talking about?" Alexander looked helplessly at Robin. Robin kept an eye on Kathleen as she came up to him and grabbed his arm.

"Robin, listen to me—it's just like I told you in the car! A premonition! You've got to be careful—someone might be trying to hurt you! But I don't know why!"

"Kathleen," Alexander said uneasily, "why don't you go lie down for a while or—"

"Don't humor me!" she snapped, turning on

him. "You don't have any idea what's going on! You don't have any idea how dangerous this could be! We've got to keep an eye on Robin every minute!"

She could hear herself, like some stranger ranting and raving from a distant place. Breaking off, she took a deep breath and stepped back from Robin. She could see him staring at her, and Alexander had a wary look on his face, and she kept shaking her head and moving farther away.

"Is it me? Does it have something to do with me? All these bad things happening to people I know—"

Again she stopped talking. Robin and Alexander were staring at each other now, and Alexander was looking mildly alarmed.

"Those pills," he said carefully, "maybe you better take some before—"

"I'm not crazy!" she nearly shouted at him. *Stop it—stop it—listen to yourself—you're freaking out —no wonder you're scaring them both to death—* "I'm not crazy, and I don't need pills. What I need is for someone to believe me!"

"I believe you," Alexander said quickly. *"Now* will you take the pills?" Once more he turned to Robin, his arms lifted at his sides. "Do *you* know?" he demanded. "Do you know what she's talking about?"

"Can you lock up?" Kathleen whirled to face Robin. Startled, he backed away from her and nodded.

"And Alexander. Can you stay with Robin? Make sure he's okay?" As the boys exchanged glances, Kathleen looked relieved. "Good. Then I'm going."

"Wait—" Alexander tried to stop her. "Going where?"

"To the police."

"Police? For a dead bird?"

Kathleen turned and went out of the room. She made her way shakily to the kitchen and got her things, then hurried out the front to the sidewalk.

What have I done? I went out of my mind. I'll never be able to face either one of them again.

She walked quickly down the pavement, hands thrust deep in her pockets, head bent against the cold. *A dead bird . . . my God . . . you're over the edge, girl. . . .*

A prank. Someone playing a joke. A sick, cruel joke. She walked faster. Her breath burned in her lungs.

If I hadn't reached up there— She suddenly stopped. *If I hadn't reached up there, Miss Finch would have.*

Miss Finch?

Kathleen stood miserably on the sidewalk and gave a deep shiver. *Miss Finch.* Maybe someone was trying to play a mean trick on Miss Finch. It was possible—most of the kids made fun of her and hated going to the library. She was always snapping at them to be quiet and not ruin the books and keep food out of the building. She was always making somebody mad. . . .

Kathleen sighed. She tilted her head up into the wind so that her cheeks stung. Maybe it didn't have anything to do with Robin. Maybe it was a twisted reference to the librarian's own last name. Besides that, Miss Finch loved birds—she had a regular aviary at home. If anyone ever wanted to get to her, a bird would be the way to do it.

"Oh," Kathleen moaned, "I can't believe I'm so stupid. . . ."

But a robin . . . and Robin . . . and after all that's happened, he's the first person I thought of. . . .

She couldn't stand it if anything happened to Robin. He was the sweetest, gentlest person she knew, and the thought of anyone ever hurting him was more than she could bear.

A coincidence, that's all it was—a bird to scare Miss Finch and nothing at all to do with Robin. And anyway . . . who would ever want to hurt him?

But who would want to hurt Bran or Della?

Kathleen frowned and started walking again. The bird had been dead a long time—who could even guess how long? It could have been lying up there for weeks. Months, maybe.

She glanced back over her shoulder. A brisk wind was blowing, and she hesitated on the pavement, eyes nervously scanning the deserted street. Shadows . . . shadows . . . more shadows . . . all restless and shifting in the wind. Wincing from the pain in her arm, she pulled her jacket tighter and went faster.

She kept doggedly to the main street. What light there was, was better here, even though most of the street lamps were either burned out or covered by trees. But as she came to a corner and started to cross the street, she suddenly stopped, her heart beating furiously in her chest.

Had that been a footstep she heard? Or just leaves blowing along the sidewalk?

Kathleen moved forward. Stopped. Listened.

There was no sound now. Only the hidden noises of the night. . . .

She ran across the street and took off down the pavement. The wind was raw in her throat, and her muscles were aching. If she could only go a few more blocks, she knew she'd reach the main intersection, with its bright lights and traffic.

She got to another corner. Dashing across the street, she heard tires squealing behind her, and she whirled into the headlights with a scream.

"Kathleen!" a voice shouted. "It's just me! Let me give you a ride!"

The next thing she knew Alexander was standing beside her, his arm around her shoulders, peering intently into her face.

"Kathleen," he said again, "come on . . . you shouldn't be walking out here alone."

With a gentle nudge, he guided her to the car.

"Did you see someone behind me?" she asked.

He gave her a curious look. He turned around, his eyes slowly sweeping the empty street.

"No. Why?

"Are you sure? Are you positive?"

Another puzzled glance. "Yes."

After helping her inside, he slammed the door and they started off.

But on an impulse, Kathleen turned in her seat.

She turned around and gazed out the back windshield . . .

And saw a shadow step into the street and watch them drive away.

12

Can I just say hi to him?" Kathleen begged.

"He shouldn't really be having visitors." The nurse gave an apologetic smile. "Doctor's orders." She hesitated, then eyed Kathleen quizzically over the top of the patient's chart. "Are you Kathleen?"

"Yes."

The nurse glanced both ways down the hall, then winked at her.

"Dr. McNally said you'd probably show up. One second. No more."

"Thanks." Kathleen grinned. She started to turn away, but the nurse stopped her.

"One thing—he knows about the accident, but we haven't told him yet about his friend. And he hasn't asked."

"They wouldn't let me see her," Kathleen admitted unhappily.

"Intensive care." The woman patted her arm

sympathetically. "I know. There hasn't been any change."

She turned back to her station, and Kathleen hurried down the hall to Bran's room.

"Bran?" she whispered.

The room was dark—only a dim nightlight burned beside the bed. She could see a form lying there beneath the blanket, but it wasn't moving.

"Bran," she tried again. "Are you awake?"

It didn't really matter that he wasn't—just standing here looking down at him was enough. Kathleen put out her hand and laid it gently against his bruised cheek. His face seemed even thinner than usual, ghostly white beneath its cuts and scrapes and bandages, yet at the same time he looked so peaceful. . . .

"Oh, Bran." She sighed.

This time his face flinched just a little. He stirred and drew a harsh breath and slowly opened his eyes.

She thought maybe he wouldn't recognize her. But then she saw that old familiar grin playing at the corners of his mouth.

"Well," he mumbled, "at least I know I didn't die and go to heaven. You're here."

"How do you feel?" She leaned close, trying to keep her voice down, her cheek gently brushing his hair.

"Probably about as good as I look."

"You look wonderful."

"Then nothing's changed."

"No." She smiled and leaned in closer, taking his hand in hers, keeping her bandaged arm behind her. "Nothing's changed."

"Where were you today?" he asked. "I looked for you."

Kathleen felt a peculiar warmth go through her. "You did?"

"Well . . . Ma did. Ma was wondering where you were."

She smiled. "Working. In fact I just got off. Alexander gave me a ride."

"Who's Alexander?"

"You know. The guy at the library last night."

Bran frowned and said nothing.

"Anyway, I was here earlier, but you weren't awake."

"No?"

"Admit it—you missed me."

He tried to look annoyed, but groaned instead. "In your dreams."

"Bran, I have to ask you something."

"So ask."

"About the book."

"What book?"

Kathleen smoothed a lock of hair back from his forehead. "You know. Right before the accident . . . you and I were getting stuff from your trunk. And I found that book."

Bran was staring up at her. He seemed confused and slowly shook his head.

"I don't know about a book."

Kathleen drew back in surprise. "But you have to. You remember—we were getting the jack and the—"

She broke off at the expression on his face. It registered absolutely nothing.

"Bran?" she whispered. "What . . . exactly *do* you remember?"

But this time his eyes just gazed back at her, huge and sad and strangely empty, and she could see him struggling to think and nothing happening. She felt his fingers move . . . felt him squeeze her hand.

"Nothing, Kath," he whispered. "Ma . . . and the doc . . . they said I got hit by a truck. But . . . I don't remember anything."

"How can that be?" Kathleen said glumly. "How can he not remember?"

"You heard the doctor." Mrs. Vanelli handed her a cup of cocoa and sat down beside her on the couch again, pulling her old, tattered bathrobe around her. "He says it's normal . . . Bran might remember . . . or he might not."

"But it's not just the wreck," Kathleen went on. "It took me awhile to realize, he doesn't even remember picking me up at the library last night."

"No"—Mrs. Vanelli shook her head—"he doesn't."

Kathleen mulled this over for several silent moments. *Bran's the only one besides me who saw that book in his trunk . . . and now it's like it never happened at all. . . .*

"Kathleen?" Mrs. Vanelli touched her hand, nudging her back to the present. Kathleen looked up with a guilty smile.

"Sorry. I drifted off."

"You shouldn't worry, *cara*—Dr. McNally says he'll be fine. This memory thing—it's a blessing, really. To shield himself from the pain . . . the shock."

"I know"—Kathleen sighed—"and in a way I'm really glad. I don't want him to know about Della."

"No, but we can't keep it from him forever. Even at the hospital there's a chance someone will say something. Bran will feel so terrible."

"When can he come home?"

"Maybe day after tomorrow." Mrs. Vanelli drained the last of her cocoa and set her cup on the coffee table. *If* we're lucky. But even then, *rest*. No visitors."

Kathleen gave a distracted nod. She didn't look forward to Bran remembering. It might prove to be way too painful.

"I've got to see Della's parents," she said sadly. "They'd already gone home tonight when I got to the hospital. I don't know if I should call them or not."

"Call them. Let them know you care."

"They probably hate me. If I were them, I'd hate me."

"Why?" Mrs. Vanelli looked shocked. "Because you were spared? You mustn't feel that way, Kathleen"—she hurriedly crossed herself—"it's like tempting fate. I mean—look at you—look what happened just tonight, falling on that glass!"

Kathleen glanced uneasily at her bandages and tried to suppress a shudder. "You're right. I'm going to call Della's mom right now."

She was glad she did. She and Mrs. Conway talked and cried, and then Mrs. Conway asked Kathleen if she could drop by for a little while. Kathleen didn't really feel up to it, but Della's mother sounded so lonely and desperate, she just couldn't say no.

"Mrs. Vanelli, I'll be back in a little while."

"What? You're going out now?"

"I have to." Kathleen sighed. "Della's mom really wanted to see me."

"I wish you wouldn't. It's so late."

"It's okay. I don't think I could sleep right now anyway."

"At least let me drive you!"

"No—really. The fresh air will feel good."

Mrs. Vanelli followed her to the door, wringing her hands. "I don't like this, you going out alone. But that poor woman—what else can you do? Tell her I'm praying—how sorry I am."

"Yes, I will."

Kathleen put on her coat and went outside. The wind had picked up, and clouds scudded across the sky. She started down the driveway when she suddenly noticed a car parked at the curb. For a split second her heart jumped, but then she recognized the sportscar and gave an inward groan.

"Kathleen?" Monica called out. "Can I talk to you?"

"What do you want?" As Kathleen grudgingly went over to the car, Monica leaned out her window. Now Kathleen could see that there were other girls in the car, too—Vivian and two more of their group—Nicole and Patsy. These three stared at her, then giggled and gave each other secret looks.

"Is it true?" Monica asked tightly. "Did Bran really have an accident?"

"Yes," Kathleen said. "He's in the hospital, and he can't have any visitors."

"We came by to see his mother. We came by before, but nobody was home."

"She's . . ." Kathleen glanced back at the house. The last thing Mrs. Vanelli needed tonight was a visit from Monica and her clones. "She's sleeping right now. Look, I really have to go."

Monica stared at her. "You need a ride?" she finally asked.

Kathleen started to say no, but Nicole flung open the back door.

"Well?" Vivian said impatiently. "We don't have all night, you know. We have important things to do!"

"Yeah," Patsy echoed. "We're off to the beach Saturday for sun and sand and gorgeous guys, right, Viv? And I have a million things to buy at the mall before then."

"Come on, Kathleen, get in," Vivian said languidly. "We all have messages for you to take to Bran."

As Kathleen reluctantly climbed into the backseat, Monica drummed her fingernails on the steering wheel. "Where are you going?" she asked.

"Bond and Seventh. Do you know where it is?"

"Nice place to visit, but I wouldn't want to live there." Vivian sounded bored. "Going to give the Conways your condolances?"

An angry reply rose in Kathleen's throat, but Monica flung the car into gear, throwing her hard against the seat.

"Hey, take it easy—" Kathleen began, but Monica cut her off.

"So is he going to be okay?"

Kathleen nodded uneasily. "Probably. We think so."

"Well, what happened?" Nicole asked. "Rumors

are flying all over the place. About Bran—*and* Della."

Like you care, Kathleen thought. But aloud she said, "There was an accident—"

Monica squealed around a corner onto a side street.

"I think someone's following us," she said suddenly. Kathleen saw her reflection in the rearview mirror and frowned. The girl looked oddly strained . . . almost nervous. As Monica redirected her attention to the road, Vivian tried to peer out the back window.

"Oh, I bet it's just Bobby," she grumbled. "You know he keeps trying to spy on you, to see if you're going out on him. Hurry up, Monica—let's lose this jerk."

Monica angled around another corner, coming back to the main road. Weaving dangerously in and out of traffic, she turned again and headed down a one-way street.

"Anyway, an accident," Kathleen said again, trying to focus on anything but Monica's reckless driving. "With a truck."

"A truck! That's not what I heard," Nicole spoke up, surprised.

Kathleen looked over at her. "What'd you hear?"

"That *you* were driving." Vivian narrowed her catlike eyes. "That you drove right into the path of another car. That everyone got hurt but you."

Kathleen felt something hot and sick rising inside her. She had to take several deep breaths before she could speak.

"That's not true. That's not what happened."

"You must feel really weird," Monica said stiffly. "With Bran and Della both in the hospital."

A stab of guilt shot through her, but Kathleen managed to keep her voice steady. "Stop the car, Monica. Let me out."

Monica braked abruptly against the curb, causing several cars to swerve around her. As the other girls watched silently, Kathleen got out and slammed the door.

"It's kind of spooky, Kathleen," Vivian purred, fluttering her fingers in a mock wave. "Sort of makes me afraid to be around you."

Monica laughed, but it sounded forced and hollow. "Especially since some pretty scary things seem to be happening to your *friends.*"

Kathleen stared at them. Then very slowly she leaned in the driver's window, her smile fixed and tight. "Then *you* don't have anything to worry about."

For an endless moment she and Monica locked eyes. She could hear Vivian saying something, but she couldn't really tell how nasty it was. The next second Monica slammed down the gas pedal and zoomed away with a shriek of tires.

Kathleen stood there on the sidewalk and tried to get herself under control. And as she stood there, she suddenly noticed the car parked down the street at the corner. . . .

A car without headlights . . .

Pulling slowly away and melting into the night.

13

It was late when Kathleen finally left the Conway house. The visit with Della's parents had been emotional, and she felt drained and depressed. After watching their pathetic attempts at normalcy, she politely refused their offer to drive her home, and instead stood waving to them as the front door closed and the porch light went off.

"Oh, Della," she whispered, "you've got to be all right . . . you've got to!"

For a minute she thought she'd start crying right there on the corner, but the sound of her own voice brought her under control. Disconsolately she started toward home.

It didn't take long to get anywhere in Fremont, but tonight she felt particularly uneasy. She kept remembering the shadow she'd seen in the street after she'd left the library, and then the mysterious car pulling away when Monica had let her out. Coincidences? In a small town like this, someone was always bound to be out walking after dark . . . and people did forget to turn on their headlights. Irritated, she tried to talk herself out of her nervousness and walked faster. *Anyway, this is a nice neighborhood with lots and lots of streetlights. What could happen?*

God, how she hated Monica and Vivian and the rest of those stupid girls. They never thought about anyone else but themselves. Even now she could still hear Monica's smug voice—*"You were driving . . . everyone got hurt but you"*—and she felt sick inside. Who could have started those lies? she wondered, and then gave a grim smile. *Monica and Vivian, of course . . . who else?*

She'd be glad when the terrible twosome left for their holiday at the beach. Better for them to be out of town till everything quieted down and got back to normal.

Kathleen sighed and crossed the street, heading for the Vanelli house. With a brisk pace, it would only take about ten minutes to get there, and the night air felt surprisingly rejuvenating. Reminders of all that had happened that day tried to creep into her mind, but she stubbornly forced them back. She wanted to believe everything was okay . . . that everything had a perfectly logical explanation. After all, things weren't always what they seemed to be—and a wild imagination could blow everything out of proportion. Bran was right. She didn't have any enemies—*except Monica, of course. Well . . . okay . . . and Vivian.*

She just didn't like the way they were always after Bran. She knew the only reason they wanted him was so they could be the envy of all the other girls.

All they cared about was his good looks and how sexy he was and how far they could get with him. They'd never take time to really *know* him—how sweet he could be, and how sincere, and how funny, and how vulnerable. . . .

But of course Bran would never see how he was being used. Monica and Vivian would totally trap him, and he'd never see it coming.

"Guys are so stupid," Kathleen muttered to herself "So . . . stupid."

It hit her then that the car without headlights might just have been some guy keeping tabs on Monica or Vivian or one of the other girls. Hadn't Monica suspected they were being followed? And by Bobby Turner, no less. Kathleen chuckled to herself. What a loser. He'd been another poor guy Monica had strung along for a few days and then dumped, and now she couldn't get rid of him.

Serves her right. Maybe the entire male student body will boycott Monica Franklin.

The thought was appealing, and it entertained her the rest of the way home. She felt almost positive as she walked up the Vanelli driveway. Bran was going to be all right, and some student was bound to get an outstanding grade with all those cutout pictures from library books, and she'd saved Miss Finch from a good scare by finding that bird on the shelf, and probably Dad had left the iron on yesterday, and life really wasn't so horrible . . .

And Della would be all right. *She has to be all right.*

She was surprised when Mrs. Vanelli met her at the door.

"It's Bran," she greeted Kathleen, giving her a hug, pulling her inside. "He's calling from the hospital—"

"Now? At this hour? Is he okay?"

"Yes, yes." She beamed. "He wants to talk to you. You see"—she winked slyly—"he's *missing* you. A mother knows these things."

"No, he probably just realized he's hungry and wants me to bring him a pizza." Kathleen chuckled. But she ran up to her room, closed the door, and eagerly snatched up the receiver. "Hi," she said. "How are you?"

"How are *you?*" His voice was soft and muffled, yet through all its layers of drowsiness, Kathleen detected a sharp note of concern.

"I'm fine," she said uncertainly. "Bran, why are you—"

"Really?" he interrupted. "Really, Kath, are you okay?"

"Why, yes, what's going—"

"Someone called here," Bran whispered.

"Bran?"

"Someone called here. A voice . . . a voice I didn't know. . . ."

"Bran?" Kathleen clutched the phone, her voice frightened now. "Bran, I can hardly hear you."

"They gave me something to sleep. Sorry . . ."

"What about the call?" And she was going cold now, cold all over. . . .

"Someone called . . . said . . ."

His voice trailed away. Kathleen shook the receiver as though somehow it would keep him alert.

"Bran, wake up! Said what?"

"Said . . . sorry, Kath . . ."

"They said they were sorry?"

"No, no . . . *I'm* sorry. . . . They said . . ."

Kathleen shook her head in frustration. She could tell he was trying so hard, yet he was drifting off . . . away from her . . .

"They said . . . your name," Bran mumbled. "And then they said . . . you're in danger. . . ."

"Me?" Kathleen said tightly. *"I'm* in danger? Bran? Bran, who was it? What did they mean?"

But there was only silence.

And then the click of the phone hanging up.

14

When Kathleen woke the next morning she felt stiff and sore, and her arm was throbbing with pain. Padding across the room, she rummaged through her purse for the pills the doctor had given her, then remembered she'd left them at the library.

Right on the desk. Great. They'll certainly do me a lot of good there.

Grumbling, she made a valiant effort to dress herself, then stumbled down to the kitchen. It only took Mrs. Vanelli one quick glance to see that she hadn't slept well.

"You're so pale, *cara!* Come—sit down. I'll fix you breakfast."

Kathleen shook her head and eased down into a chair. "I can't. Really. Just coffee, please."

Mrs. Vanelli bustled to fill her cup. Then she pushed some homemade pastries across the table with a coaxing smile.

"If you change your mind. They're your favorite."

"Thanks." Kathleen gave a wan smile. "Maybe later."

"Yes, yes, later." Mrs. Vanelli crossed herself and leaned over to pat Kathleen's hand. "Everything will be all right. You'll see."

"You look nice today," Kathleen told her. "Where are you off to?"

"First to church to pray for poor Della. Then to the hospital to see my boy." At the mention of Bran, Mrs. Vanelli beamed proudly. "You'd like to come with me?"

"Could you drop me at work afterward?"

"I'm a regular taxi service!"

When they got to the hospital, they went immediately to intensive care to check on Della. There'd been no change through the night, and Mr. and Mrs. Conway were in the waiting room, looking haggard and worn. For a moment Mrs. Vanelli stood in the doorway watching them, then she turned to Kathleen with an anxious frown.

"I'll speak with Della's parents. You go on—tell Bran I'll be up in a little while."

Kathleen nodded, relieved to escape. If she stood there a second longer, she was afraid she'd start crying.

Bran was lying in bed with his head turned to the window. He didn't respond when Kathleen slipped into his room, and for a moment she thought he hadn't heard her. But then, as she moved closer, she noticed the way his shoulders suddenly seemed to tense, and how he wiped a hand quickly across his eyes as she stopped beside him.

"Bran?" she whispered.

He kept his face turned away.

"They told me," he said tightly. "They told me about Della."

Kathleen's heart wrenched. She opened her mouth, but nothing came out. Groping across the covers, she found his hand and squeezed it.

"Have you seen her?" Bran asked.

Kathleen swallowed hard and tried again. "There's no change. Your mom's with her parents now."

Bran's cheeks flinched. He closed his eyes, his whole body struggling for control.

"It wasn't your fault," Kathleen told him helplessly. "Didn't they tell you how you tried to save her?"

For a long while he said nothing. When his voice came out at last, it was so low that she had to lean over to hear it.

"I don't remember."

She squeezed his hand again. She could see his throat working furiously as one tear finally slipped out and trailed down his cheek.

"Oh, Bran," she choked. She slipped her arm around him and held him tightly. He didn't pull away. Instead he pressed his cheek against hers and made a muffled sound in his throat.

Kathleen didn't know how long they stayed that way, locked together in their fear and grief. It was Bran who finally pulled away, clearing his throat and shifting on the pillows, putting distance between them.

"Yeah, well," he said gruffly, "so when can you get me outta here?"

In spite of herself she had to smile. "I wish all the girls could see you now. Stitches all over your face . . . black and blue marks. I guess they wouldn't think you're so cute now, would they?"

"Cuter. Shows my macho side."

"Umm. You and Frankenstein."

"Very funny." He tried to smile, but grimaced instead. "So can you smuggle me in a pizza?"

"I knew it. The only thing you ever think about is your stomach—"

"Well . . . not the *only* thing—"

"Sorry, but they don't allow that in hospitals, so you might just as well keep your hormones under control." She stood off from him and frowned, shaking her head. "What a mess you are. But maybe—*maybe* if you're nice to me—I could bring you something later on."

Bran looked bored. "Yeah, but will I like it?"

"You're terrible. I don't even know why I bother with you." She reached over and tousled his hair, which she knew he hated. "Just remember—you're trapped in that bed, and I could do *anything* I wanted, and you couldn't do a thing about it."

"I could call the nurse."

"She'd just help me."

"Sounds kinky. Go ahead."

"Look, I have to go to work pretty soon, so could we please talk about our phone conversation last night?"

Bran sighed. "What phone conversation? What happened to your arm?"

Kathleen automatically put her bandaged hand behind her back. "I tripped on some broken glass at the library—"

"Yeah, that sounds like something you'd do—"

"The phone conversation, Bran," Kathleen said, trying to steer the discussion back again. "You remember. When you called home last night and told me about the warning."

"What warning?"

Kathleen gave a short laugh. "Bran, come on, stop kidding around."

"I'm not kidding." He turned his head toward her on the pillow, and her heart melted. With his bandages and bruises he looked so vulnerable . . . almost childlike. "What are you talking about?" he asked.

"Bran"—Kathleen took a deep breath—"you called home last night. Your mom talked to you, and so did I."

He looked confused. "I did?"

"Yes, you did."

"And I said what?"

"You said someone had called you—here—at the hospital and told you I was in danger."

His face was blank. It came to her then that he was honestly trying to think, but his face winced in pain. Slowly he shut his eyes.

"Oh. That," he mumbled.

Kathleen looked relieved. "Yeah, that."

"I must have been telling you about my dream."

"Your dream?"

He closed his eyes, lay there for a minute, opened them again. "I don't know . . . they keep giving me stuff to make me sleep. But . . . yeah . . . I had this weird dream. I dreamed the phone rang . . . and I picked it up . . . and then this voice said 'Kathleen's in danger.'"

Watching him, Kathleen shivered. "When did you have this dream? Before or after they gave you sleeping pills?"

Bran shrugged. "I don't know."

"And the voice? You didn't recognize it?"

"It was a dream, Kath."

"A dream? You're sure? It wasn't real?"

"No, it was a dream. I'm pretty sure."

"Bran," Kathleen said slowly, "a minute ago you swore you never called home, even though your mom and I both talked to you. So how can you be so sure the person who called was a dream?"

He looked troubled. "Kath, why would anyone say that? And why would they call me here in the hospital? Does that make sense?"

"No, but not many things have been making sense lately." She sighed. "Bran, are you *sure*—"

"Kath, what happened yesterday?" He rose up in bed, propping himself on his elbow, his eyes turned pleadingly into hers. "All anyone'll tell me is that there was an accident."

"Yes, but you're okay." She put her hand lightly on his forehead, trailed it slowly down the side of his cheek. "And I have to go to work. Bran, if it was a dream . . ."

He groaned. "It was a dream—"

"Then why would you dream something like that? Why would you dream that someone was warning you about me?"

"I don't know, Kath." He sounded almost angry now. "I guess 'cause subconsciously I'm still freaking out over this accident I don't remember."

"Okay, okay," she said, trying to soothe him. "Get some rest, all right?"

"Will you come back?"

"Of course. Just as soon as I get off work."

He nodded. He shifted restlessly, his head falling back onto the pillow, his eyes closing shut. She stood and watched the rise and fall of his chest beneath the covers. After several moments she could tell he was drifting off again.

A soft knock sounded at the door. An aide slipped in, handed Kathleen a basket of flowers, then went back out to the hall. For a long moment Kathleen stared at the gift card. Finally she pulled it out and began to read the message.

FORGIVE ME. I NEVER MEANT TO HURT YOU.
                                    LOVE, MONICA

"Bran . . ." Kathleen whispered.

He didn't move.

With trembling fingers, she tucked the card back into the basket.

Then she leaned over, kissed his cheek, and left.

"Robin?"

The library was so cold.

"Robin, where are you?"

Kathleen walked around turning on lights, turning up the thermostat, knowing it would do little good. The wind had picked up, and the old building shuddered with every blast.

"Robin?"

She glanced at the clock, frowning. For once she was on time—a little early, in fact. Robin probably just hadn't gotten here yet, that was all. Nothing to worry about. . . . She put a pot of coffee on and took a cup back with her to the front desk. Then she sat down and took another look at Miss Finch's list.

This dumb thing . . . there's no way I'm ever going to get all this done before she gets back. What does she think I am, a machine?

Kathleen sighed loudly, running her finger down the paper. Filing, shelving, ordering, transferring, sorting through catalogs, calling people about special requests, organizing everything in the reserved section, finding information in the reference section, not to mention helping Robin with the new room whenever she had a free minute.

"Free minute?" Kathleen grumbled. "Get a life, Miss Finch." She paused, then almost laughed out loud in spite of herself. "Oops, sorry, Miss Finch, I forgot. The library *is* your life."

She bent down once more, squinting in concentration. She read down the paper, then groaned and shook her head.

She couldn't stop thinking about Bran's phone call.

A dream . . . but he wasn't really sure. . . .

Then who had called him? And if it really *was* a dream, why had he dreamed about her being in danger? Bran had no way of knowing about all the strange things going on—the broken window, the dead bird, the shadow in the street, the car without headlights . . .

But you promised yourself you wouldn't think about those things anymore. . . . You figured out they all have perfectly logical explanations that have nothing to do with you.

Still . . . she wished Robin were here. She

thought again about the nursery rhyme impaled on the dead bird, and she tried to shake her growing uneasiness. *You're making something out of nothing. . . . Stop scaring yourself.*

She got up and went to the book drop, reluctantly sorting through the titles as she carried them back to the counter. At least there wasn't anything unusual this time. *I can't believe this—I'm getting paranoid about everything.*

She was bent over the list again when a hand touched her shoulder, and she jumped straight out of her chair. Robin jerked back from her, eyes wide with surprise.

"Oh! Robin!" Kathleen collapsed against the desk, her hand to her heart. "Oh, I'm sorry—you just—I'm just—"

She stared at him, then burst out laughing.

"Robin, you look more scared than I do! Where *were* you?"

He gestured in the direction of the children's room.

"I called and called—didn't you hear me?" she demanded.

He shook his head, looking contrite, then offered her a tentative smile. At last Kathleen smiled back, her voice softening.

"Look, I know I'm acting kind of weird lately, with everything going on. You remember the stuff I told you in the car yesterday?" At his nod she added, "Well, there's more. Last night after I left here."

She told him about her feelings of being followed . . . the shadow in the street . . . the ride with

Monica . . . the car without headlights. She finished with Bran's phone call and how he hadn't remembered anything this morning at the hospital.

"So what do you think, Robin?" she asked unhappily, reaching to take his hand. "You think I'm crazy?"

They stood there quietly side by side, but then, after several moments, Kathleen felt him shift and move closer. He was facing her now, their bodies lightly touching, so that she could feel his chest and stomach beneath the worn softness of his shirt.

"Oh, Robin . . ." Kathleen sighed. She felt his hand upon her hair, stroking it gently. She looked up at him and saw his wide dark eyes so full of concern. "Why do I always feel so safe with you?" she asked him.

A faint smile went over his lips. His hands slid down each side of her face . . . lingered at the sides of her throat . . .

The front door blew open.

Jumping back, Kathleen saw several people come into the library, and Robin stepped away. After a quick glance in the newcomers' direction, Robin turned and disappeared through the door and into another room.

The morning went quickly. Kathleen had more than enough to keep her busy, hardly stopping to eat their takeout pizza at noon. It wasn't till after five that the main room finally emptied, and Kathleen decided to take a break, wandering through the other rooms to see how many people were still in the library. Going upstairs to reshelve some books, she passed the Fremont Collection

Room and was surprised to see Alexander hard at work. She hadn't even seen him come in today.

At first she didn't speak. She tiptoed up behind him and saw that he was bent over a notebook, crossing words off a list. She leaned in closer, but before she could even whisper, the notebook snapped shut and he whirled around in his chair.

"Don't do that!" Kathleen's breath came out in a rush. "You could have given me a heart attack!"

"I could have given *you* one?"

"I didn't know you were studying—how long have you been here?"

"Hours and hours."

"I didn't see you downstairs."

"You were busy being a librarian. I didn't want to interrupt."

"You could have said hello," she grumbled, and Alexander looked amused.

"You're right, and I stand corrected. How are your friends?"

Kathleen sighed and pulled up a chair. "Bran's better, but he's still really confused. He doesn't even remember the accident. He found out this morning about Della, and that was a big shock, of course. She's still unconscious. They won't even let me see her, but I talked with her parents last night."

Alexander reached over and covered her hand with his own. "I'm sorry," he said again, more sincerely this time.

She gave a tired nod. "Are you finding everything you need?"

"Even more than I bargained for. I had no idea the collection was this extensive."

"Most people who live here don't realize it, either," she admitted with a chuckle. "The town's pretty boring now, but it wasn't so boring back in Civil War days." She stood up and smiled. "Want some coffee?"

"Am I allowed to have anything in here?"

"No, but you can join me at the desk."

"I'd be honored."

She finished her rounds, then met him in the front room. Alexander took the cup she offered and sat down on the edge of the counter, stretching his long legs out in front of him. He had on jeans and a T-shirt, with a loose denim shirt over that, hanging open at the front. One shock of hair fell stubbornly over his forehead, and his glasses had slipped to the end of his nose.

"So how's the project coming?" she asked him, and he nodded, obviously pleased with himself.

"Wonderful. I've got a good feeling about this paper."

"So what was so private up there that you couldn't let me see?"

Alexander held her in a level gaze. "Just a list of topics I still have to look up."

"From the way you jumped, those must have been top-secret topics."

His look didn't waver. "You surprised me, that's all. I hate being sneaked up on."

Kathleen watched him a moment, then shrugged. "So spring break hasn't been a total loss?"

His glance traveled quickly from her head to her feet. "Not a loss at all."

Kathleen looked away. Alexander took a long sip of coffee.

"Kathleen," he said seriously, "I know you haven't known me very long. But if you ever want to talk, you can. I mean, you seem like you're carrying an awful big load of worry. I'd like to listen if you need me to."

His gaze locked on some bookshelves at the other end of the room. He twirled his cup slowly between his fingers. Staring at him, Kathleen felt herself weakening—suddenly she wanted to blurt out everything, to tell him all her fears and worries, no matter how stupid and unreasonable they seemed. She opened her mouth, but before she could say a word, she noticed Robin silhouetted in one of the adjoining doorways. As she turned in surprise to get a better look at him, he vanished.

Kathleen frowned and shifted her attention back to Alexander. "It's been . . . a bad week," she finally said.

He nodded. "So I gathered."

Tell him. Tell him about the book in Bran's trunk . . . tell him about the phone call Bran thinks he dreamed last night . . .

"You're still upset, aren't you?" he ventured carefully. "About the window, I mean."

She didn't answer, only looked down at her bandaged arm and hand.

"But you can see how it happened." Again he sounded cautious, reluctant to upset her. "And the bird. You know, at one of the libraries where I worked, we were always finding dead birds lying around. They got in through cracks up in the attic, then came out again through the old ventilation system. Nobody could ever catch them to take them back outside."

She shrugged her shoulders, sighing. "I think someone might have left it there for Miss Finch's benefit. She loves birds, and that would really have sent her over the edge."

"You know," Alexander went on calmly, "once you start blowing things out of proportion, then *everything* gets distorted. One thing naturally leads to another."

Kathleen gave him a tight, forced smile. "Yes, you're right. That's exactly what happens."

He smiled at her then and drained the last of his coffee.

"Well," he said, "I'd better take off. I've got that drive back to Brookside, and lots of things to do tonight."

"Oh. You have a date?"

Instantly Kathleen flushed. It was none of her business—after all, she didn't care anything about his social life.

"As a matter of fact," he said slowly, standing up and stretching, "I don't. I was referring more to laundry and homework and getting to the cleaners before they close. Do you feel sorry enough for me to go get a bite to eat?"

She looked surprised. "Me?"

Alexander glanced around. "I don't see anybody else in here. It *must* be you."

"I have to work till seven."

"Perfect. That'll give me time to do a few errands and change. I'll pick you up here?"

"That'd be great." She thought a minute, then frowned. "But I wanted to see Bran at the hospital before visiting hours are over."

"Bran again."

"Not Bran again!"

"Joke. Only a joke. I'll run you by there myself and wait for you."

"Really?"

This time he sighed and headed for the stairs. "You're not too trusting of people, are you? I said I would."

"And you'll give Robin a ride home, too?"

Alexander paused on the bottom step. "Why not? Can you think of anyone else who might need chauffeuring?"

Shaking his head, he continued upstairs to get his things. Kathleen picked up her list, then put it down again with a smile. She didn't know why she felt happier, but she did. Alexander was really cute, especially when he wasn't being quite so solemn. The thought of spending the evening with him made her smile again.

In a few minutes he came back down and told her goodbye. Kathleen watched him go out the front door—so calm, so sure of himself, so unbothered by things—and suddenly she felt more peaceful than she had in days. *He's right. You imagine one thing, and then everything else gets blown completely out of proportion.*

She settled down again behind the desk, feeling almost at peace.

Then she remembered Della.

She remembered the truck, and the way Bran had thrown himself into the street trying to save Della's life as the huge wheels rumbled toward them—

"Stop," Kathleen choked. "Stop it!"

How could she possibly go out for something to eat with Alexander tonight—how could she even *think* about having fun when Bran and Della were lying in the hospital . . . ?

The minutes dragged by. She wanted to call Alexander and tell him she wouldn't be able to go after all, but she didn't know how to reach him. Searching through the collection of phone books on the desk, she found a number for Brookside Student Directory and dialed. The line rang and rang. *Spring break,* she reminded herself. *No one's going to be there to answer the phone.* She'd just started to hang up when someone finally answered.

"Hi," Kathleen said. "Could you please give me the phone number for Alexander Hodges? The third?" she added.

The girl wasn't amused. She sounded as though she very much resented having to answer the phone at all. "Phone number? Phone number . . . where would the phone numbers be. . . . Okay. Hold on."

There was a long wait. In the background Kathleen could hear a radio playing . . . the muffled sounds of typing. Then the phone being picked up again.

"He's not here," the girl said bluntly.

"Not—" Kathleen broke off, puzzled. "Are you sure?"

"Sure," the girl retorted. "No number for Hodges. Goodbye."

"Wait," Kathleen tried to stop her before she hung up. "Wait, please. Is he even registered at Brookside? Is he a student there?"

"I don't know," the girl said. "I don't know about any of that stuff."

"Well, who does?"

"You'll have to call back. Nobody's here."

"When will someone be there?"

"Look, I'm only filling in for spring break. I don't know where anything is, and I don't know how to help you, okay? Now, goodbye."

Kathleen stared at the phone in her hand, listening to the dull sound of the dial tone. *No number?* Of course that didn't mean anything, not really—a lot of students didn't have telephones. . . . Still, Alexander seemed like the kind of guy who would definitely have a phone. . . .

Kathleen put the receiver down and slumped back in her chair. *Not registered there? Now, don't go doing it again—making mountains out of molehills—the girl said herself that she didn't know anything, and anyway, why would Alexander tell you he's a student if he's not?*

I'll just ask him, Kathleen decided. *Tonight when he picks me up. The whole thing's silly anyway. That dumb girl didn't know what she was talking about—*

She reached for the phone again and called Mrs. Vanelli to tell her she'd be late getting home. There was still no news about Della. She dialed once more and called the hospital, but when the operator put her on hold and forgot to come back, she got mad and hung up.

Seven o'clock came at last. She locked the front door, then went systematically through all the rooms, straightening up, turning off lights. It occurred to her that she hadn't seen Robin all evening, and she wondered where he'd gone.

"Robin?" she called. "Robin, Alexander said he'd give you a ride home, so come on out!"

But Robin didn't answer.

Room by room, Kathleen kept on, trying to find

him. But every room was empty. No late stragglers browsing through books . . . and no Robin.

Funny . . . he never just leaves at night without letting me know. . . .

"Robin!" An edge of panic crept into her voice. She walked faster, hurrying through the empty rooms, eyes nervously probing the drafty aisles and dark corners. The library loomed large and shadowy around her, and she rubbed a growing chill from her arms. "Robin, come on—where are you!"

There wasn't a sound. It came to her then that she might actually be all alone in the building, and she desperately fought to stay calm. *What's the matter with you? Just lock up and get out of here, you're a big girl. . . .*

And then she thought of the bird. The dead bird and the strange message impaled on its lifeless chest. *Come hither, sweet robin, and be not afraid. . . . I would not hurt even a feather. . . .*

"Robin!" she screamed. "Do you hear me? I'm leaving now—I'm locking up! So you'd better come on!"

She was almost to the kitchen now. She started through the doorway, and then she froze. Robin was standing at the sink with his back to her, and as she came in, he straightened up and hurriedly wiped his hands on his red flannel shirt.

"Oh, God, Robin, there you are." Kathleen's breath came out in a rush. "You scared me half to death—I didn't know what to think! Where were you?"

He made a vague motion that could have meant anywhere at all. Kathleen went to the closet and got her coat and purse.

132

"Listen," she said impatiently, "Alexander said he could give you a ride home."

Robin shook his head. His sleeves were rolled up past his elbows, and his jeans were splattered with dark stains. He wiped his hands again, and as Kathleen looked more closely, she could see faint streaks of red on his wrists and forearms. Frowning, she glanced behind him and saw a tin of red paint and a paintbrush on the counter. Robin hastily put the lid on and stuck the brush beneath the faucet.

"Oh." Kathleen nodded her approval. "You've been painting the children's room. No wonder you didn't hear me at first." She buttoned her coat and said again, "Alexander can give you a ride if you—"

Robin stepped away from her. He turned off the water, grabbed the can and brush, and went out the back door. For a long moment Kathleen stood there staring. The door stayed closed, and Robin didn't return.

Kathleen let out a deep sigh. She should have known better—Robin just didn't feel comfortable with people he didn't know—she should have realized he'd be too shy to ride with the two of them. Smiling a little, she went out onto the porch, but Robin had disappeared. The night was so dark . . . so still except for the wind. The alley lay before her, swarming with restless shadows. Uneasily she locked the door, then walked through the gloomy old building and let herself out the front.

A car was parked at the curb.

Kathleen hurried toward it, then began to slow down. . . .

Alexander?

She couldn't tell from here, it was too dark. The car was just a mass of shadows among many.

Kathleen went closer . . . squinting . . . trying to see.

If it *was* Alexander, he looked like he was sleeping, angled there in the shadows with his head leaned back against the seat.

"Alexander?" she called softly.

He didn't answer.

Kathleen crossed the last few feet to the car. She could see now that his window was open, and she walked up beside it and leaned in slowly so as not to startle him.

And then she saw what was in the front seat.

As her hands flew to her mouth, she stumbled back, trying to get away, but her eyes wouldn't move, and she had to keep looking, even though she wanted so much to run—

It wasn't Alexander, and it wasn't his car.

Monica sat there behind the wheel, her head flung back, her hands arranged neatly in her lap. . . .

She was holding a book.

Phantom of the Opera.

And as Kathleen screamed and screamed, all she could see was the blood . . . and the horrible blisters . . . on Monica's beautiful face.

15

She didn't remember getting back to the porch.

As Kathleen flung open the door and fell into the library, all she could see was that hideous thing out there in the car. It hadn't even looked human—if she hadn't seen the long blond hair, she wouldn't have recognized Monica at all—

She stumbled to the phone and somehow managed to dial 911. She didn't know what she was saying—if she was even making sense. She slammed the receiver down again, then shrieked as a hand closed over hers.

Kathleen whirled, swinging out with the telephone. She caught Alexander in the side of the head, and as his face went slack with surprise, he staggered backward, catching himself on the corner of the desk.

"Alexander! Oh, my God!"

"Take it easy!" He held out both hands to ward her off. "It's me, Kathleen, calm down."

"Oh, Alexander, I'm so sorry!"

Bursting into tears, she felt his arms slip cautiously around her. Then he held her close, rocking her gently against him.

"What is it?" he whispered. "What's going on?"

"Didn't you see her—didn't you see!" And she kept pointing, kept pointing toward the door while he just stood there, staring down at her, not understanding. "Out there—Monica—"

Alexander glanced uneasily over his shoulder. "I saw a car. Who's Monica?"

"She's *out* there—her face is all—I don't know! Burned—bleeding! I think she's dead—"

He drew a sharp breath and pushed her firmly back against the wall. "Stay right here."

"I just called the police—Alexander, where are you going? No, don't go out there!"

She grabbed him and held on. Alexander tried to disentangle himself, then looked up again in frustration as they heard sirens in the distance.

"Alexander," Kathleen babbled, turning him around, forcing him to look at her, "it happened again! The book, and the—the message—only this time it was Monica. Someone's sending messages with books, don't you see?"

"What are you *talking* about?" he mumbled.

With one firm thrust he pulled free, then hurried outside. The sirens were getting closer now. As Alexander raced down the sidewalk, Kathleen followed, but stood back when he yanked the door open on Monica's car. She saw him reach inside . . . hesitate . . . then lightly feel the pulse point on Monica's neck.

"She's alive," he said. "Barely."

But Kathleen was staring. Staring past him and staring down, into the front seat of the car.

"Alexander . . ." she whispered.

"Acid," he turned toward her, a stony look on his face. "Someone used acid on—"

Kathleen grabbed him, digging her fingers into his arm. "Alexander, listen to me! The book's gone!"

"What book?"

"The book she was holding! Do you hear me— it's gone!"

He stared at her. She was backing away from him, lips moving soundlessly, and as he reached out for her, she sidestepped his grasp.

"Kathleen," he said sternly, "what the hell are you *talking* about!"

"It was here . . . I saw it. . . ."

"You're not making any sense!"

The first police car pulled up, sirens wailing. An ambulance followed. Kathleen saw the whole thing as in a dream . . . people moving in slow motion . . . shadows whirling around her . . . voices mumbling questions . . .

There were quite a lot of questions.

But very few answers.

"There's nothing else you can think of? Any possible link, no matter how small," Alexander said. He took a bite of his hamburger and chewed it slowly. Kathleen stared down at her Coke and shook her head.

"I've told you all there is to tell. I've told the

police all there is to tell." She lowered her head, resting it in her hands. "I can't answer any more questions, I'm all talked out."

"But that part about the book—"

"They didn't believe me." She sighed. "And you don't, either."

"I didn't say that."

"You were thinking it. She was holding a copy of *Phantom of the Opera*. She *wasn't* holding it when the police got there."

"And in the book the Phantom had been disfigured with acid." Alexander nodded glumly.

"I didn't imagine it. The book was *there.*"

He chewed again thoughtfully. He wiped his mouth on a napkin and spread his hands out on the tabletop.

"Then where did it go?"

"The same place *Inferno* went. The same place *Anna Karenina* went. Now do you see why I'm so upset? What about Robin and that dead bird? What if something happens to Robin next?"

"I thought we decided this afternoon that the bird has nothing to do with anything—"

"I couldn't stand it if something happened to Robin!"

"Nothing's going to happen to him. I mean, think about it. Did he look upset when you found the bird? Has he been acting scared for his life?"

"Just because he doesn't take it seriously doesn't mean something couldn't *happen!*"

"Okay, okay, you're right," Alexander said, trying to soothe her. "But if you want my honest opinion, I don't think you have to worry about Robin. And I appreciate the fact that you sat here tonight and told me about all these other things that have been happening. But—"

"But you think I'm crazy."

"I didn't say that. I admit . . . these accidents *seem* . . . convenient. They *seem* like a lot more than . . ."

"Coincidences?" she returned defensively.

"Don't do that," Alexander scolded. "I'm not the bad guy here, okay?"

Kathleen leaned back in the booth. She crossed her arms over her chest. "You're not listed in the student directory at Brookside," she told him.

Alexander stared at her. "I know that. Have you been checking up on me?"

Her cheeks reddened. She looked down at her plate.

"I'm a part-time student," Alexander explained calmly. "And I don't live on campus. And the room I'm renting doesn't have a phone. What is this, anyway?"

She said nothing. She gazed so hard at the table that her napkin and food and silverware began to merge into one blurry pattern in front of her eyes.

"I'm scared," she said softly.

For a moment there was silence. Then Alexander reached across the table and touched her hand.

"You tell me all this now . . . but you didn't tell the police. Why?"

"Because they'd laugh at me." Her eyes filled with tears, and she quickly blinked them back. "Wouldn't you? If someone came in talking about these books that don't exist? I have to live in this town."

He seemed amused by that. He smiled softly,

then withdrew his hand and leaned back into the corner of their booth. "Do you want my opinion?"

"Do I have a choice?"

"Of course you do. But I think it's wise right now that you don't tell them about the books." He hesitated . . . drew a deep breath. "Kathleen . . . when they got Monica out of her car tonight, you saw what happened . . . didn't you?"

Kathleen nodded. She'd seen it, all right, just as clearly as she'd seen the book. Only the book had disappeared, but when everyone had been standing there—Alexander, the police, the paramedics— something *else* had fallen out of Monica's lap when they'd pulled her out.

"Yes," she mumbled. "I saw it. Her purse was in her lap when they took her out. But"—she leaned across the table, her look pleading—"I saw what it was when I found her. And it wasn't her purse. It was a book."

He didn't say anything. His brow furrowed, and he seemed to be carefully choosing his words.

"And you don't think . . . that in your frame of mind . . . maybe it just looked like a book? And when you saw her face, somehow—I don't know how—that title came into your mind?"

"Right, Alexander," she said bitterly. "Whenever I see some horrible tragedy, the first thing I think about is fiction imitating life. Give me a break."

He nodded and held up his hands. "You're right, you're absolutely right. And I'm sorry. But *that's* why I don't think you should go to the police with this."

She lowered her head again, feeling hurt and

angry. Across from her Alexander toyed absently with his napkin, brushing it back and forth through the water rings on the table. At last she looked up at him, her voice very small.

"What kind of person would do something like that?"

He shook his head, his face a mixture of sadness and disgust. "One with no conscience."

"But . . . *how?*"

"A person with no conscience is capable of anything."

Kathleen shuddered. In here were lights and crowds and music . . . out there beyond the windows were darkness and drizzle and the unknown.

"So could it really mean that some maniac is loose in Fremont, stalking people?"

"That's not what the police think," Alexander said. He picked up his cup and took a sip of coffee. "I guess that's one advantage you have of living in a small town—they already seemed to know a lot about Monica. You heard what they said—she has plenty of enemies—both guys and girls. She's obviously made a lot of kids jealous and angry and unhappy. It could have been anyone."

"Nobody here would do something like that."

"You can't be sure. How well can you ever really know someone, anyway? This person could even be a friend of hers . . . or somebody she thought was a friend."

"You're scaring me."

"I don't mean to, I just want you to be careful." He thought a moment, then said, "You didn't much like her, either, did you."

"No," Kathleen admitted guiltily. "But that doesn't mean I'd ever wish something like this on her."

He nodded and sighed, glancing down at his watch. "Look . . . it's too late to see your friend at the hospital now. Why don't you let me take you home."

"Yes," Kathleen agreed, pushing away her uneaten food. "Maybe that'd be best."

She hated to leave the restaurant. She hated to leave the noise and the warmth . . . the comfort of Alexander's presence. Reluctantly she let him help her on with her coat and lead her outside. Together they walked through the parking lot. Ragged clouds slithered over the moon, and Kathleen stood there, watching the sky, while he unlocked her door.

"All I can think about . . ." she murmured at last, and Alexander leaned close, trying to hear her.

"What? What is it?"

"All I can think about . . . was how Monica was leaving this weekend for spring break. She and Vivian and some other girls were going to the beach." Kathleen drew a deep breath, her voice breaking. "If they'd only left sooner . . ."

"Come on, you can't think about that. Think about the fact that you probably saved her life by finding her when you did."

"But maybe . . . if I'd gone out there sooner—"

"Hey . . . stop . . ."

Alexander's arms went around her. Instinctively Kathleen stiffened, but as he pulled her close, she felt herself lean willingly into his embrace. They stood there for a long while, his face lowered, one cheek resting against the top of her head. Hesitantly she slipped her arms around his waist and laid her head on his chest, and then, very gently, his hand slipped beneath her chin, tilting it upward to meet his kiss.

It was a long kiss . . . warm and soft . . . and when it finally ended, Kathleen closed her eyes and held him even tighter, her heart beating out of control.

His hands slid slowly down her back . . . sending shivers up her spine. As Kathleen caught her breath, she straightened in his arms and gently pushed him away.

"I think," she mumbled, "you should take me home now."

Alexander nodded and opened her door "I think that's an excellent idea."

She was still trembling as she got in the car. Alexander slid in on the other side and put the key in the ignition. He didn't turn it on, and she didn't ask him to. They sat there in the darkness without speaking. The street lamp angled down through the windshield, casting their faces in half light, and as a tear rolled down Kathleen's cheek, Alexander reached over and took her hand.

"Kathleen . . . I'm sorry if I—"

"No." She shook her head. "No, it's not you."

"Then what? Bran?"

"Bran?" That surprised her. She glanced at Alexander and shook her head. "No, of course not Bran. I don't know—just everything."

He moved sideways. His arm went around her shoulders, drawing her close. She could smell the wool of his jacket and the faint scent of aftershave, and she braced herself, not wanting to feel any more emotions.

"He'll be taken care of, you know," Alexander whispered.

Kathleen started. She shifted and looked up at him, bewildered. "What? What are you talking about?"

"Bran." Alexander's eyes flicked to hers, then away again. "You did tell me that, didn't you? That he's going home soon? Where he'll be taken care of?"

Kathleen stared at him. "Yes. Probably tomorrow."

"Tomorrow," Alexander echoed. He slid behind the wheel and turned the key. "Things always look different tomorrow."

16

Mrs. Vanelli hadn't heard about Monica yet.

Shocked by the news, and that Kathleen had been the one to find the girl, she sat up late with Kathleen, talking and trying to make sense of it all.

"She acted kind of strange when she gave me a ride," Kathleen told Mrs. Vanelli. "Nervous . . . sort of on edge. I think she was really upset about Bran." For a split second the gift card flashed through her mind, and she stared blindly at the TV screen. She hadn't wanted to think about its meaning—hadn't *allowed* herself to think about the message all day.

I NEVER MEANT TO HURT YOU. . . .

"Upset about Bran," she mumbled, and she fiercely shut her mind against the memory of Monica's flowers. "The last time she and I talked, we were mean to each other."

"You were angry, *cara*," Mrs. Vanelli said, trying to comfort her. "Don't think about that—we say lots of things we don't really mean when we're upset."

Kathleen nodded miserably. She hugged her arms around her chest and snuggled deeper into the sofa cushions. Mrs. Vanelli moved her chair closer and gently stroked Kathleen's hair.

"And no one saw anything tonight?" she went on anxiously. "No one heard anything?"

Kathleen shook her head. "Alexander got there right after I found Monica. He saw the car out by the curb, but he didn't think anything about it."

"And what about poor Robin?"

"He'd already left. And anyhow, he goes the back way—through the alley in the opposite direction. He wouldn't have seen anything out in front."

"I just can't believe it." Mrs. Vanelli sighed, shaking her head sadly. "Who could do this to a young girl? I just don't know."

A person with no conscience, Kathleen wanted to say, Alexander's words ringing in her ears. But instead she changed the subject.

"How was Bran tonight?"

Mrs. Vanelli nodded, looking sly. "Sulking."

"Sulking? Why?"

"'Cause you never went by to see him."

"He said that?"

"Of course he didn't say that. A mother just knows these things."

Kathleen hid a smile. "I'm sure he never noticed."

"Trust me, *cara.* Nothing but *you* could put him in such a sorry mood. Why don't you call him? Look—here's the phone number in his room." She slid a scrap of paper across the table as Kathleen glanced at the kitchen clock.

"It's so late now," Kathleen said. "I'll see him tomorrow. He *is* coming home?"

"He is, and I've got his room all ready." Mrs. Vanelli beamed. "I'm getting balloons! And baking his favorite cookies."

In spite of everything, Kathleen chuckled. She could only imagine what it would be like around here tomorrow, with mother and son at each other's throats again.

"And what about Della?" she asked reluctantly.

"Still nothing. Nothing." Mrs. Vanelli patted her shoulder encouragingly. "It will take time, *cara*. Maybe many weeks. We don't give up . . . we never give up."

Kathleen was glad to escape to bed. She felt frightened and confused, and she couldn't keep her thoughts in any kind of order. She kept seeing Monica's face . . . the burned and blistered flesh. She kept hearing Vivian's nasty remarks and the screech of the tires as Monica tried to outrun that other car.

She kept feeling Alexander's kiss . . . his embrace . . .

Kathleen flushed, going weak all over. She wished she could call Bran just to hear his voice, but she knew he'd probably be sleeping, and she didn't want to disturb him.

Bran . . .

Funny that Alexander had mentioned him tonight—and at such a moment. As if she and Bran were involved somehow and serious about each other. Lying there in bed, the idea almost made her laugh. And yet . . . she wished Bran were with her now. . . .

She'd always been able to talk to Bran when she was upset—able to talk to him about anything. It had been like that since they were little kids. They'd played together, had terrible fights and arguments, and been best buddies. They knew each other's secrets and worst fears and just which buttons to push to make the other one react. They'd had other friends and dated other people and been close and drifted apart and sometimes deliberately ignored each other. Yet none of that had mattered—she'd always known Bran was there, no matter how different or busy their lives had grown.

Kathleen swallowed a lump in her throat. Mrs. Vanelli was right, of course—if she went away to school this fall, it would be the first time in their whole lives that she and Bran would be separated. And then what would happen? She supposed they would write . . . even call sometimes . . . but their worlds would be totally different, their visits few and far between. How would that feel? Kathleen wondered. She couldn't begin to imagine.

She laid one arm across her eyes, shifting restlessly on her pillow. An image of Bran's face flashed into her mind—his eyes . . . his grin . . . the way he teased and laughed and could drive her completely crazy like no one else could. How had it happened over the years, and right under her nose—Bran going from the class clown to the sexy guy every girl wanted?

Her eyes brimmed with tears. She closed her eyes and tried to block everything from her mind. After a long while she finally began to doze, her head swirling with vague impressions, not quite dreams . . .

Bran's face began to melt . . . to fade. It was Robin now she was seeing, and even in her twilight state, she felt a cold stab of fear in her heart. She saw the page from the book of nursery rhymes. . . . She saw the dead bird. . . .

Moaning softly, Kathleen turned over on her side, nestling her cheek into the pillow. Robin was smiling at her, and his smile was fading, just like Bran before him, and it was Alexander floating there now, eyes peering intensely behind his glasses. His face came closer . . . closer . . . and suddenly he was kissing her, touching her, and she wanted him to, yet she was trying to get away—

She felt his lips on her neck . . . pressing the sensitive spot at the base of her throat . . . only it wasn't Alexander anymore—it was Bran—and she clung to him as her heart exploded and she cried out his name—

Kathleen bolted upright in bed. Her gown was damp with sweat, and she was gasping for breath. Eyes wide, she looked at the window and saw that it was still pitch dark outside. Without stopping to think, she turned on the lamp and reached for the scrap of paper on her nightstand. Then she dialed the number and waited for him to pick up.

"Huh?" Bran said fuzzily. There was a muffled thump as he dropped the phone, and she could hear him fumbling the receiver. "What?"

"It's me," she answered.

There was a momentary pause, then, "So?"

"So how are you?"

"So what do you care?"

Kathleen smiled. For some reason, just hearing his voice made her suddenly feel all mixed up, like laughing and crying at the same time. She took a deep breath and tried to keep her voice steady.

"I'm sorry I wasn't there tonight."

"Yeah? So where were you?"

Alexander's kiss . . . Alexander's touch . . . Kathleen cleared her throat, suddenly defensive. "I was busy."

"Yeah, like I believe that."

Kathleen took another breath. She stared at the covers heaped around her. "It's just that . . . a lot's been going on."

There was a silence. Then Bran said softly, "You mean . . . like Monica Franklin?"

"How'd you know about that?"

"Vivian came by and told me."

Kathleen didn't know what to say. As she shut her eyes and bit down on her bottom lip, her stomach did a queasy turn.

"She did?" she said at last. "Your mom didn't tell me."

"Ma wasn't here."

"Oh." She groped for words. "She . . . I saw Monica sent flowers. They came while you were asleep and—"

"Those were from her?"

"Of course they were from her. Didn't you read the note?"

"What note? There wasn't a note. What'd you do with it—since you obviously read it?"

"She said—that is, she wanted to tell you—" Kathleen stammered, but Bran's voice cut her off.

"Kath," he said seriously, "what's going on?"

"I . . ." She opened her eyes again. She stared at her hand clutching the phone. "What do you mean? I just wanted to see how you were."

"At three in the morning? It's three in the morning, Kath."

"Is it? Oh, goodness. My watch must have—"

"Kath, cut it out. I can see you, so don't play around with me."

"Oh, you can, can you? And who are *you?* The Great Vanelli with X-ray vision?"

"You're sitting there in bed under all those covers, with your knees pulled up to your chest— the way you always do when you start sounding defensive and think you're fooling me—"

"You don't know what you're talking about—"

"And your hair's all messed up, hanging down over your shoulders, except for that one piece that always kinda curls out to the side, and you don't have any makeup on—"

"Yuck. Please stop—"

"—so naturally you look like Godzilla in a nightgown—Ma's nightgown, by the way—the yellow one that makes her look like a grapefruit—only you look much better in it—"

"Thanks a lot."

"And your eyes are kinda wet, and you have that look—you know, that look on your face . . . the sad one . . . 'cause I can tell you're trying really hard not to cry. . . ."

His voice trailed off. Kathleen turned her head from the phone, so he wouldn't hear her sniffle. The silence dragged out. She drew a shaky breath and put her mouth near the receiver once more.

"Kath," Bran said gently, "don't you know by now you *can't* fool me? Don't even try."

She swallowed hard. She wiped one hand slowly across her eyes.

"I miss you, Bran," she whispered.

Again there was silence.

For one awful moment Kathleen thought he'd hung up.

Then, "Yeah," Bran mumbled. "Yeah, Kath. I miss you, too."

17

She slept soundly after that—a deep, peaceful sleep without dreams. When she finally woke up, she lay there in bed, watching another gray morning dawn beyond the windowpane. Her conversation with Bran last night seemed more like a fading memory now. She thought about the way it had ended and shook her head with an amused smile. He'd been delirious, obviously. Bran would never have admitted any sentimentality to her unless he'd been under the influence of hospital drugs.

Mrs. Vanelli was in her room on the telephone when Kathleen went looking for her. She was shaking her head and clucking her tongue sympathetically, and as Kathleen sat down on the edge of the bed, Bran's mother rolled her eyes.

"No, but I'll ask," Mrs. Vanelli said into the mouthpiece. "Hold on." She covered the phone with her hand and hissed at Kathleen, "Have you heard from Vivian Wenner?"

Kathleen shook her head. "No. Why?"

"It's her mother on the phone. Vivian didn't come home last night."

Kathleen stared at Mrs. Vanelli. A cold tingle started up her spine, but she firmly shook it off.

"The poor woman." Mrs. Vanelli looked genuinely distressed. "Vivian and her friends were supposed to leave for the beach this morning, but nobody's seen her."

"She went to see Bran at the hospital sometime," Kathleen offered reluctantly.

"She did? And when was that?"

"I don't know—he said you weren't there."

"He told you this?"

"Yes. When I called him last night."

Looking even more worried, Mrs. Vanelli turned her attention back to the phone. Kathleen gazed down at the nightstand, her heart sick and heavy. She heard Bran's mother hang up . . . heard her sigh loudly as she shut her closet door.

"She didn't come home last night," Bran's mother said again. "They haven't seen or heard from her. Both Mr. and Mrs. Wenner were at a party and came home late. They didn't check Vivian's room until this morning when her friends called."

Kathleen raised her eyes. Mrs. Vanelli shook her head sadly.

"Her bed hadn't been slept in. Her poor parents have called the police."

This time Kathleen couldn't hold back a chill. "Don't they have any ideas? Maybe she's with some *other* friends—or—or a guy. Or maybe she's shopping or something."

Mrs. Vanelli nodded. "I just wonder if she's gone off somewhere to be alone. It makes sense—Monica was her friend, after all. Maybe this is something she has to do, to deal with the shock."

"Sure." Kathleen forced a grim smile. "I'm sure that's it."

"The police say they have to wait," Mrs. Vanelli went on. "They can't do anything right now—she hasn't been missing long enough. . . ."

She left the sentence unfinished. Kathleen twisted her hands together in her lap. *But in the meantime she could be in danger . . . could be hurt . . . could be . . .*

"Well!" Mrs. Vanelli said firmly. She took a last look in the mirror, patting her hair into place. "I'll fix your breakfast. And then I'll go to the hospital and get my boy."

"No, don't make anything," Kathleen insisted. "I'll grab something later."

"Hmmph! Something not healthy for you, I bet my life on it."

Kathleen got up and kissed her on the cheek. "As if all your Italian pastry and sauces could be healthy for me!"

"And listen to you! You're starting to sound just like Bran!"

Chuckling, Kathleen followed her downstairs. Mrs. Vanelli dropped her off at the library, and as Kathleen went up the walk, she was surprised to see Alexander standing in the open doorway, smiling at her.

"Hi," she said, surprised. "What are you doing here?" A quick flush went over her face at the memory of last night, and she turned her head, annoyed with herself.

"Waiting for you. You're late."

She glanced at her watch, then back at him. "Only ten minutes. How'd you get in?"

"Robin," he said. "Did you know he's very good at prying things loose? He got the basement window open, came up here, and unlocked the door."

Kathleen shook her head with a smile. "That doesn't surprise me."

"Meaning?"

"Meaning, Robin can do anything. Build anything . . . fix anything . . ."

"You think a lot of Robin, don't you?"

Squeezing past him into the room, she gave Alexander a curious glance. "Yes, I do. He's a very special person."

"And the feeling's more than mutual."

"Why do you say that?"

"It's not hard to figure out." Alexander raised an eyebrow. "Just the way he looks at you."

"Robin's my friend," Kathleen said, brushing off the comment. "He looks at everyone that way. He's just naturally sweet."

"He's different with you," Alexander kept on, following her. "I can see it. I imagine he'd do anything in the world for you."

"He'd do anything in the world for anyone," Kathleen insisted again, more firmly this time. "If they needed him to."

"I thought you said he wasn't comfortable around people."

"He's not. But that doesn't mean he wouldn't

help someone if they were in trouble." She headed toward the kitchen to put her coat and purse away. All the lights had been turned on, but the rooms still felt damp and chilled. "Where is he, anyway?"

Alexander shrugged. "I don't know. He let me in, and that's the last I saw of him."

"Robin!" Kathleen called. "Robin, are you here?"

Her voice sounded strange in the quiet. She listened, but there was no answer.

"He's probably working in the west wing." She sighed, then turned and looked squarely at Alexander. "I'm really worried about Vivian Wenner."

Alexander looked back at her, bewildered. "Who's that?"

"A friend of Monica's."

Alexander was watching her closely. At last he gave a slow nod and waited for her to go on.

"Her mother called Mrs. Vanelli this morning. Vivian didn't go home last night."

Alexander lowered his head. He rubbed his fingers over his chin, deep in thought.

"If something bad happens—" Kathleen began, but he held up a hand to silence her.

"Does anyone have a *reason* to think something bad's happened? Have they checked with all her friends? Boyfriends? Maybe she ran away."

"Remember how I told you a bunch of them were going to the beach this morning? Well, she never showed up."

"So maybe she left all by herself. Maybe she went to a big party last night and spent the night somewhere else. Maybe"—he drew a deep breath—

"she went off alone to work things out about her friend."

Kathleen gave a halfhearted nod. "That's what Mrs. Vanelli said. I hope so. I hope . . ."

She closed her eyes for a brief moment. She opened them again when she felt his hand on her arm.

"Look, Kathleen, I know what you're starting to think, but just stop it right now. Whatever's going on doesn't have anything to do with you. Just like that girl in the car last night had nothing to do with you."

"But all those other things—the things I told you about—"

"The things that had nothing to do with you, *either!* Come on, I thought we agreed to forget about all of it." Alexander sounded almost impatient. "This girl—Vivian—there could be a million reasons she didn't go home last night. And if this had happened at any other time, you probably wouldn't even be giving it a second thought."

Kathleen swallowed hard . . . nodded. "I guess you're right. . . ."

"She'll show up," he said. "In the meantime, stop turning everything into something symbolic. It just *happened.* Things do."

Kathleen crossed her arms over her chest. She chewed her lip and looked down at the floor.

"Really," Alexander insisted, more kindly this time. "It's not your responsibility—*or* your worry. Now, I'm going up to work." When she didn't reply, he reached over and touched her lightly on the arm. "Friends? Truce?"

Kathleen barely nodded. After watching her for several more seconds, Alexander squeezed her arm, then left her alone in the room.

He's right. I've got to stop this. I'm turning myself into a complete wreck.

She went out to the desk and got busy. Saturdays were always slow at the library, but today was even worse. The hours dragged by torturously, and Kathleen kept watching the clock, wondering if Bran was home yet, wondering about Della. She was half tempted to close early if things didn't pick up around here—she figured Robin wouldn't mind, and she could always tell Miss Finch there'd been trouble with the electricity or heater or something.

She was going through some files when the phone rang. Picking up the receiver, she balanced it on one shoulder with her chin and kept on working.

"Fremont Public Library, may I help you?"

"Is Vivian there?" the voice asked.

Kathleen froze. She saw her left hand on the papers in front of her . . . her bandaged one resting on top of the file cabinet. She felt her heart skip a beat.

"Excuse me?" she said hesitantly.

"Is Vivian there?" the voice spoke again . . . a soft, muffled voice, barely above a whisper.

Chills raced up her spine. She clutched the receiver in her fist and leaned slowly, slowly into the phone.

"This is the library," she said, trying to sound cool and professional. "Who did you want to speak—"

"Vivian." There was a pause, then the voice hissed, "You know Vivian. You can read her like a book."

And the room was spinning, and her voice came from a long way off—

"Who *are* you?" Kathleen whispered. "Why are you *doing* this?"

The line went dead.

Kathleen slammed the phone down and spun to face the room. She could see several people in the aisles, their heads bent over, browsing. She could hear feet shuffling . . . an occasional sniffle and clearing of throats. Forcing herself to stay calm, she left the desk and went deliberately through every room on the first floor, up and down each row of bookshelves, past every table and chair. She raced upstairs, poking her head into each room there, startling people, startling Alexander, who turned and looked at her quizzically over the top of his notebook. Then she rushed down again, and out the front door, out onto the sidewalk, looking frantically up and down the deserted street.

Nothing.

No sign of Vivian Wenner . . . no sign of anyone.

Kathleen fought down a wave of panic and went back inside.

"Robin!" she called. "Robin, come here—I need you!"

She didn't care that she was making noise and annoying people—she didn't care if Miss Finch heard about it or not. Growing more frightened by the minute, she went into the west wing and made a hurried search. She couldn't find Robin anywhere, even though it looked as if he'd been working recently. *Where is he . . . ? He's got to be here some-where. . . .*

Kathleen stopped at the children's room.

She stopped and looked carefully at the wall-to-wall chaos—the tools and trash, the canvases and clutter. She chewed nervously on a fingernail and tried to think what to do. The room looked even creepier today. Tilting her head, she breathed deeply of the stale air, then slowly backed away. Was it only her imagination that there seemed to be a faint odor lurking somewhere beneath all the paint fumes and mildew . . . a strange odor . . . one she couldn't quite identify. Whatever it was, it was definitely unpleasant, and after another quick glance around, Kathleen turned and left.

A prank call. That's all it was. Just someone making a prank call . . . probably one of those stupid girls in Monica's car last night. . . .

"You can read her like a book. . . ."

It doesn't mean anything. . . . I've already decided that none of it means anything, none of it has anything to do with me. . . .

She went back out to the front desk.

She stood there behind it and lowered her head into her hands. She was trembling all over, and the coldness inside of her had faded, leaving a sick, hot feeling. She felt flushed and slightly dizzy, and she straightened again and headed for the bathroom. Maybe if she got some cold water to put on her face . . . maybe that would make her feel better. . . .

The bathroom was tiny and claustrophobic, and since it was the only one in the building with halfway decent plumbing, it was used by everyone.

As Kathleen walked inside, she caught a glimpse of herself in the mirror and stared at her pale reflection. *I've got to stop this. I really do have to let go of all this right now.* Locking the door behind her, she leaned over the sink and let a thin stream of water run slowly over a paper towel. She pressed it against her forehead and cheeks, closing her eyes as pain throbbed at her temples. She turned off the tap and dried off, and then as she started to go out again, she saw the book.

It was lying on top of the old radiator against the wall.

It was lying there, slightly angled, so that from where she stood, she had no trouble at all seeing the cover and the title printed there in big, bold letters . . .

Kathleen reached out for the sink. She gripped the edge and held on tightly as her knees went weak and a small cry escaped her lips.

"No," she whispered, "no . . . no . . ."

She didn't want to touch it.

She didn't want to pick it up or hold it or take it back with her to the desk, but the letters were so *big,* and the title leaped off the cover straight at her, that one word screaming over and over into her brain—

KIDNAPPED.

18

Somehow she got the door open.

She got the door open, and then she snatched the book up from the radiator and went running through the building—

She got to the front desk and tossed the book onto the counter, and as she grabbed up the telephone to call the police, a hand came down on her arm.

Kathleen jumped back with a scream. To her dismay, a little boy stood there glaring at her, his face puckered in a fierce scowl.

"Hey," he said, "that's my book. Give it here."

"What?" she mumbled. "What book? What are you talking about?"

The boy's scowl deepened. As he flung out his arm and pointed at the book on the counter, Kathleen slowly replaced the receiver and stared at him.

"That's my book!" the boy said again. "You can't take it! It's mine!"

"What do you mean, it's yours?"

"What I said! I left it in the bathroom, and now I want it back! So give it to me!"

Kathleen watched helplessly as he yanked it out of her grasp. Her mind was whirling so fast, she couldn't think. *Then it is a mistake—it was a prank call—and the book was just a coincidence and doesn't have anything to do with anything—*

She watched as the kid stormed out the door, then she glanced sheepishly around the room. Several heads popped back behind bookshelves, not wanting to be caught eavesdropping, and those few people standing nearby shrugged sympathetically. Flushing, Kathleen held her head high and tried to make a dignified exit.

She went into the kitchen and poured herself a cup of strong coffee. She stood at the back door and watched the steady downpour of rain, the trees lashing in the wind, the darkening masses of clouds.

"Hey," said a voice behind her, "what's going on?"

Kathleen started and turned around. Alexander's face wore its typically solemn expression, and his eyes shifted slowly from her to the gloomy scene outside.

"Are you okay?" he spoke again, more cautiously this time. "I thought I heard someone yelling."

"You did." Kathleen said with a sigh.

When she didn't go on, Alexander shrugged. "Well?"

"I just put my foot in my mouth," she grumbled. "Big time."

"Would it have anything to do with you running around upstairs a while back?" he asked mildly. "With a crazed look on your face?"

"Sort of." Kathleen leaned back against the door and frowned up at him. "Did I look crazed?"

Alexander smiled. He put his hand on her shoulder and squeezed lightly. "Very. You should win an Oscar for the way you burst into the room. So . . . do you want to tell me about it, or do I have to guess?"

Kathleen shook her head. She stared down into her coffee cup and then up again at him.

"I think . . . thought . . . Vivian was kidnapped."

If Alexander was surprised, he didn't show it. His face remained calm and controlled, and his head inclined slowly as he stared at her.

"The reason being . . ." he prompted.

"The reason being that someone called the library and asked to speak to Vivian and said something about a book." Kathleen's tone was defensive. "And then I found *Kidnapped* in the bathroom, so naturally I thought . . ."

Her voice trailed away. She looked back at Alexander and made a futile gesture with her hands.

"What about the bathroom?" He looked confused.

"The book. *Kidnapped.*" Kathleen tilted her head back and banged it gently against the door-frame. "Stupid . . . *stupid!* I'm so stupid! I thought whoever it is that's been causing these accidents—

leaving these clues—left it there because of Vivian!
The voice on the phone said, 'You can read her like
a book.' But the book belonged to some little boy,
for God's sake—"

"Okay, calm down. You made a mistake, that's
all, that's not a crime. Don't be so hard on yourself.
After all that's happened, it's natural for you to—"

"Don't patronize me," Kathleen said. The words
came out more harshly than she intended, and
Alexander looked as surprised as she felt. "Sorry."
She sighed again. "This hasn't been one of my best
weeks."

She slammed her cup down on the counter, then
plopped into a chair, leaning forward to cross her
arms on the table. She rested her chin on top and
regarded him in total bewilderment.

"I mean, what else could I have thought? They
asked to speak to Vivian. They said she was here,
then they said I could read her like a book. Why
wouldn't I have thought it was some kind of clue?
Vivian didn't go home last night—Vivian is *missing!* What was I *supposed* to think!" She made a
frustrated sound deep in her throat. "I started to
call the police! That's all I could think about—to
call the police and warn them before it's too late!"

She closed her eyes briefly. When she opened
them again, Alexander was drawing up a chair and
sitting down next to her.

"Too late for what?" he asked quietly.

"If you have to ask that, then you're crazier than
I am," Kathleen said, annoyed. "Before whoever
has her *hurts* her! *Kills* her! *Hides* her away forever!"

"Maybe," Alexander said carefully, putting out his hands as though to ward off an expected attack, "Vivian was *supposed* to be here today. And maybe someone knew that and was trying to get in touch with her."

"She was *supposed* to be going with her friends to the beach for spring break! God, why won't anyone listen to me!"

"I'm listening, Kathleen, I'm just trying to—"

She didn't wait for Alexander to finish. She got up from the table and went back to the main desk. She sat down and started shuffling papers back and forth and tried to pull herself together. *Easy . . . easy . . . you're okay . . . don't fall apart now. . . .*

She heard throats clearing behind her. She whirled around and saw a small group of people waiting to be checked out. Apologizing profusely, she tried to smile and act normal as she chatted and went quickly through the line. The last person had just gone out the door when Alexander approached from the other direction and stopped beside the desk.

"I've done all I'm going to do today. How about having dinner with me?"

Kathleen gave him an embarrassed smile. "I'm sorry I acted that way back there in the kitchen—"

"No, it's okay. You don't have to be sorry."

"And I'd really like to have dinner, only I can't. Bran's getting out of the hospital, and I've got to get home."

Alexander sighed. "Ah, yes, Bran again. I see."

"It's nothing like that," Kathleen said quickly. "It's just that his mom might need help and—"

"You don't have to explain. I understand perfectly."

"No, I don't think you do—"

"As a matter of fact, I'm sure I do."

His lips moved in a faint smile. His voice was
matter-of-fact. As Kathleen watched in confused
silence, he hoisted his books beneath his arm and
walked away.

The door closed loudly, its hollow sound going
back and back through musty rooms. The library
was empty now, and unnervingly quiet. Kathleen
looked at the clock on the wall. Five—time to close
up. But where was Robin? She'd been looking for
him all day without any luck, and it just wasn't like
him to disappear this way. . . .

Even her breathing seemed to echo. Her footsteps were unnaturally loud as she walked across
the floor. Maybe he'd run some errand and been
delayed. Maybe he'd gotten sick after he let Alexander in this morning—maybe he'd been home all
day. *But he would have left a note. . . . He would
have let me know so I wouldn't worry. . . .*

She didn't want to lock up till she found him. Or
at least till she was convinced he wasn't still here
working somewhere. A million things could have
happened, she argued with herself—it wasn't like
she expected him to keep her informed about every
detail of his life. If he'd had to leave, she was sure
there was a good reason for it. And maybe he *had*
tried to find her, but hadn't been able to, and was in
a terrible hurry. . . .

Still . . . that's just not like him. . . .

She told herself not to panic. She refused to let

herself think of the dead bird and the nursery rhyme. *Just remember what Alexander said . . . about giving significance to things that don't mean anything. . . .*

Thinking of Alexander took her mind momentarily off Robin. If she didn't know better, she'd almost think he was upset about her seeing Bran tonight. As if that meant anything at all. Why did Alexander keep implying things about her relationship with Bran? It was totally ridiculous . . . childish, even. And what did Alexander care, anyway? He didn't believe anything she said—he thought she was stupid and crazy, she was sure of that. *Well, good riddance,* Kathleen thought angrily. *Who needs you, Alexander Hodges the third?*

Irritated now, she made her usual rounds of turning off lights and picking up books and checking to see if anyone was still in the building. She thought about the phone call . . . the book on the radiator in the bathroom. Again Alexander's words crept into her mind, though she tried hard to block them out—*"Maybe Vivian was supposed to be here today. . . ."*

Back at the desk again, Kathleen picked up the phone book and flipped through to the *W*'s. She found the Wenners' number with no trouble and scribbled it on a memo pad. She hadn't planned on doing this, hadn't planned it at all. So it surprised her when she suddenly realized she'd dialed the number and was waiting for someone to pick up on the other end.

"Mrs. Wenner?" she asked gently when Vivian's mother answered. "Hi . . . this is Kathleen Davies.

I was just . . . you know . . . wondering if you'd heard anything yet. About Vivian."

If she'd expected tears and hysterics, she was sadly mistaken.

"No, we haven't, and we need to keep this line open," Mrs. Wenner said crisply. "I'm going to ground her for the rest of her life when she comes home."

Taken aback, Kathleen stared down at the receiver in her hand. Then she managed to stammer, "I'm so sorry. I'm sure she'll be back soon—she's probably just so upset about what happened to Monica and—"

"Nicole calls this morning to tell me Vivian hasn't shown up! She and the other girls are there— *waiting*—and all of them are furious! So I tell Nicole, maybe Vivian got held up at the library."

"The . . . the library?" Kathleen mumbled.

"All I did was have her go by the library to drop off my books. Is that too much to ask? And Vivian says to me, she'll *think* about it! She says to me—"

"Mrs. Wenner," Kathleen cut her off, "are you saying Vivian was supposed to come by the library this morning? Before she left on her trip?"

"Well, *I* didn't have time to do it!" Mrs. Wenner exploded. "I was supposed to be at the club today, to help with a luncheon! Of all days for her to pull a stunt like this—this is the third time in two months that she's sneaked out! And frankly, I'm getting pretty sick of it! Hello? Hello?"

Kathleen's hand shook as she hung up the phone. So Vivian *should* have come by the library this morning . . . and someone *could* have called trying to find out if she was here . . . *but that part about the book—that part still doesn't make any sense. . . .*

A cold draft whispered along the floorboards. Kathleen shivered and walked slowly to the center of the room. Shadows oozed from corners . . . down narrow aisles . . . along rows and rows of dusty books . . .

"Robin!" Kathleen called again. "Robin! Are you here? I'm going home now—I'm closing up!"

He must have left, she reasoned with herself; otherwise he would have responded long ago. Going into the kitchen, she collected her things and suddenly remembered the basement. The door was standing slightly ajar, and as Kathleen stared at it, a slow feeling of dread began to creep over her.

Maybe he fell . . . got hurt . . . hasn't been able to answer . . .

She opened the door, went down three steps, and listened. There were no lights on below, and she couldn't hear a sound. After standing there a few more minutes, she came back up and secured the latch.

It was so quiet . . .

Too quiet . . .

Even for the library.

Once more Kathleen felt a deep chill move up her spine. Was it her imagination, or had it gotten even colder in here the last few seconds? *That stupid heater . . . must be going out again. . . .*

She looked again at the basement door. She hadn't even considered the possibility that Robin might have hurt himself while he was working.

Now she pictured him lying somewhere, hurt—lying there alone all day, waiting for her to find him, unable to call for help. The very thought of it made her feel sick inside, and she hurried to the west wing to make another search.

The rooms were like caverns, huge and yawning and empty, oozing mold and rot from every dark corner. She tried not to look and kept her eyes averted, heading straight for the area where Robin had been working. There were few lights back this way—what switches worked illuminated only bare, single bulbs in the high ceilings. As Kathleen passed through the connecting doorways, windows rattled in their frames, and dampness blew in through the cracks, fluttering cobwebs that clung to the walls.

"Robin? Robin, are you back here?"

She'd almost reached the last room when she heard the sound.

A long, drawn-out groan . . .

For one split second she thought it was human, and the hair lifted slowly along the back of her neck.

But then, as the groan ended with a muffled thud . . . she realized it was a door closing.

Kathleen fought off a wave of panic. Turning around, she retraced her steps back through the rooms to where she'd first come in.

And she could see it now, the door that led into the main room of the library—she could see that it was closed, and she chided herself for not having thought to prop it open. Grumbling to herself, she gave it a push.

The door stayed shut.

Surprised, she pushed again, turning the knob, twisting it back and forth.

It took her a few minutes to realize the truth of her situation.

She was locked in.

19

Hey!" she screamed. "Somebody get me out of here!"

Her words echoed back at her, cold and taunting.

There's nobody here but me . . . I can't even find Robin.

She tried the knob again—beat on the door with her good hand.

"Dammit!"

In desperation Kathleen made a fist. She slammed it furiously against the wood, then recoiled with a cry of pain. These doors to this wing were thick and made of solid oak—it would take a battering ram to break them down.

"Oh, God, I've got to get out of here. . . ."

Helplessly she turned and faced the room behind her. In the distance she could hear the muffled ringing of a telephone, and her heart sank. What if that was Alexander calling to ask her to dinner one more time? Or Mrs. Vanelli asking when she'd be home to see Bran?

She could picture the telephone—could see it as clearly as the walls rising around her—could see it sitting right there on the front desk, ringing and ringing, right there beside the lamp, right there not twenty feet away from the front door of the library and a way out.

Was there an extension?

Kathleen tried to think. She could almost remember Miss Finch saying something about putting a phone back here, so that when she was working with Robin, she wouldn't have to run all the way out to the front to answer a call. . . .

Kathleen hurried back toward the children's room. If she didn't get that phone, there was no telling how long she'd be locked in here. Surely Mrs. Vanelli would start worrying when she didn't come home tonight. Surely someone would come looking for her before tomorrow. . . .

Her eyes made a quick survey of the room as she walked in. No phone outlet . . . at least not that she could see. She went over to the window where she'd cut her arm. Robin hadn't fixed it yet, and rain was coming in, spraying across the floor. On impulse Kathleen reached up and shook the bars. Then she leaned her forehead against them and tried to think what to do.

She couldn't hear the phone anymore. Whoever had been trying to call must have given up. Kathleen was aware of something scurrying across the floor behind her, and she slowly turned around. Roaches, probably, or mice . . . maybe even rats.

Robin always had a real problem getting rid of the pests, even though Miss Finch insisted. He hated hurting things . . . killing things. Kathleen had no doubt this whole building was infested with vermin —it surprised her that any of the books were in decent shape at all.

I can't spend the night in here. . . . I can't spend another minute in here.

Shuddering, Kathleen tried to think. A window seemed to be her only hope of escape—if not in this room, then maybe in another. Maybe she could find one where the bars were loose—maybe she could even manage to pry them apart and squeeze out.

She looked around hopefully for some kind of tool she could use. It was growing much darker in here now, and rain beat hard against the window-panes. The air was so damp and heavy, it was hard to breathe.

Slowly her gaze went over the walls and floor-boards. Lumber . . . bags of nails . . . paint cans . . . brushes . . . drop cloths . . .

Her eyes settled reluctantly on the drop cloths.

They lay around the room in shapeless lumps, crumpled and stretched like loose strips of skin. Kathleen shuddered and moved slowly to one corner. She could see a crowbar there, and as she breathed a sigh of relief, she bent to pick it up.

Her foot slipped in something wet.

Something wet and greasy seeping over the floor.

Startled, she jumped back, then bent to examine it more closely.

There was a puddle there, smeared now from the sole of her shoe.

A dark . . . thick . . . gluey puddle . . .

That seemed to be oozing from under the drop cloth.

Kathleen's heart nearly stopped.

She felt her lips move as she tried to tell herself this wasn't really happening, and she felt her hand reach out in slow motion to lift one corner of the cloth. . . .

She saw his eyes first.

Wide and glassy and staring right at her.

And then, as she started crying, as she started talking to him—*get up please get up why are you looking at me like that for God's sake please get up*—as tears streamed down her face, she saw the cloth sliding away and the hideous thing protruding from his chest . . .

The twelve-inch metal file rammed through his shirt—

The other bloody holes in his clothes—on his face—where it had struck again and again . . .

Kathleen screamed.

She screamed until there was no other sound but her rage and her grief.

And then, as she put one hand to Robin's chest, as she watched his blood stain her palm and her trembling fingertips, she suddenly froze.

Somewhere a door was being opened.

Its creaking sound echoed back through the rooms.

And down the hall . . . closer and closer . . . came footsteps.

20

She was going to be sick.

She gagged and clutched her stomach and scrambled into a corner.

She cowered there in cover of shadows, and as lightning flashed off and on beyond the windowpane, she could see Robin's eyes staring at her . . . then disappearing . . . then staring again . . . as though begging her for one more chance at life.

She'd never been so terrified.

She realized she'd dropped the crowbar, and she could see it lying there on the floor only three feet away, but she was too scared to crawl over and get it.

The footsteps came closer.

They came slowly . . . hesitantly . . . stopping . . . starting again.

Kathleen held her breath. Her heart felt ready to burst.

As a glow of lightning slithered through the room, she saw a shadow silhouetted in the doorway, and she put a hand to her mouth to hold back another scream.

"Kath," the voice whispered, "are you in here?"

"Bran!"

She was in his arms in an instant, clinging to him, crying, as he held her tightly and tried to calm her down.

"Bran! Oh, Bran—"

"Shh . . . shh . . . come on, what's the deal here? Yeah, it's me . . . are you okay? What're you doing back here in the dark?"

"The bird"—Kathleen gasped—"it happened just like the killer said it would—"

"What bird? What are you talking about?"

"Robin! Someone killed Robin!"

And she was pulling him toward the other wall, where the dropcloth lay all askew, and as Bran saw the familiar figure sprawled there on the floor, he drew a slow, stunned breath.

"Oh . . . oh, my God . . ."

Kathleen stood back as Bran knelt beside the body. Slowly he put one hand to Robin's neck and felt for a pulse. Without warning, Robin suddenly began to move, and as Kathleen watched in horror, she saw his head turn and his hand slide down onto Bran's arm.

Kathleen couldn't even scream—her eyes were riveted on Robin. As in a nightmare, she could see his fingers tightening on Bran's sleeve, and Bran's look of anguish as he leaned in close to Robin's face.

A strange sound came from Robin's throat.

Blood trickled from the corner of his mouth and bubbled from the hole in his chest. . . .

To Kathleen's amazement, she saw his lips move. And then . . . one word struggled out.

"Danger . . ."

Bran recoiled as if he'd been struck. His face went pale, and as he groped for Robin's other hand, he leaned in even closer.

"It was you," he murmured. "Not a dream. That night at the hospital . . . someone *did* call me on the phone . . . but it was *you*, wasn't it?"

Robin's head moved slowly. He was fighting for breath.

"You were trying to talk," Bran went on urgently, "only I couldn't understand you. You were trying to tell me . . . trying to save Kathleen . . ."

Robin squeezed Bran's fingers.

There was a gurgling sound, and his eyes went wide.

They smiled at Kathleen.

Bran didn't move. His head was bent . . . his shoulders trembled.

Very carefully he pulled his hand from Robin's.

"He's gone, Kath," he whispered.

She could hear him talking to her, yet he sounded so far away. . . .

"Kath. Kath! Come on, let's get outta here!"

But she could only stand there, staring down at Robin's face—the wide open eyes still smiling—

"Kath!" Bran gabbed her and gave her a shake. "He's dead—we can't help him!"

"He was gone all day," she mumbled, "and I didn't know—if I'd looked for him like I should have—if I'd gotten help—"

"Jesus, Kath, come on!"

He dragged her through the doorway, and she had no choice but to follow. She felt peculiarly robotlike, with no thoughts or will of her own. She could still see Robin's eyes . . . the eyes of the bird on the library shelf . . . both of them, both of them impaled and dead. . . .

"No." She tried to hang back, tried to twist out of

Bran's grasp, and she could hear herself getting hysterical, her voice rising and rising through the dreary, dead rooms—"No, not Robin, no—"

"Kath, for God's sake, shut up!"

Bran slapped her. She felt the sharp sting across her face, and as she stared at him in stunned silence, he grabbed her and held her and let her cry.

"I know, Kath, I know, but look, we need to get outta here, you understand? Come on, don't fall apart on me now!"

He held her at arm's length . . . gave her another shake. After several moments Kathleen finally nodded and pulled away. She hurt all over. As she wiped her tears and stared at Bran, she realized that he was struggling hard not to cry himself.

"I've never seen anybody dead before," she whispered.

"Me, neither. Blow your nose."

"I don't have anything to blow with."

Bran frowned and glanced around the room where they were standing. Spotting a rag on the floor, he picked it up and handed it to her.

"What's this?" she sniffled. "It's all dirty."

"So's your face. Just use it." He took her elbow and steered her along beside him. Kathleen could see now that he was limping badly, and she put a restraining hand on his arm.

"Bran, you're hurt. You shouldn't be walking on that leg."

Bran shrugged off her concern. "Doc says my leg might be bad for a while—it's no big deal."

"What are you doing here anyway? How'd you get in?"

"I told Ma I wanted to see you, so she dropped

me off. You *did* leave that book by my bed, right? As a joke?"

"What book?"

"Sleeping Beauty."

For a second the room seemed to recede around her. Kathleen put one hand on the wall to steady herself as she stared at him.

"Vivian," she mumbled. *"That's* the book. Not *Kidnapped* . . . it was *Sleeping Beauty*—"

"Kath, what are you *talking* about?"

"Vivian's dead," she said flatly. She could see Bran looking at her, his face a mixture of bewilderment and fear.

"What?" he demanded. "What does Vivian have to do with my book? I walked up to the visitors' lounge, and when I came back, somebody'd put this stupid book by my bed. I thought it was you."

"It wasn't me."

Bran nodded . . . glanced nervously back over his shoulder. "After Ma let me off, I tried to get in, but the doors were locked. I went around to the back and looked in the window. I could see your stuff on the table, so I figured you were still here."

"I couldn't get out of the west wing," Kathleen explained. "And there's no phone back there. And I forgot to prop open that stupid door."

"Well, when I couldn't see you, I started getting worried. I tried looking in a few more windows around the side. I thought it was weird that Robin wasn't around—it's like he's always looking after you."

Bran paused, his eyes on the floor. He swallowed a few times, then went on again in a low voice.

"I found a loose window in the basement and

came up that way. But I still couldn't find you. Then I thought I heard this noise—like somebody walking around—so I tried to be real quiet, and I came back here."

They were at the door now, the one leading out to the main part of the library. To Kathleen's relief it was standing wide open, and Bran pushed her through.

"We gotta call the police, Kath. We gotta find who did this to Robin."

"It's just that I've been trying so hard to tell everyone," Kathleen mumbled. "Only nobody will listen to me. Nobody will believe me—"

Bran turned on her in frustration. "Kath, cut it out, okay? You're talking in riddles here—I don't understand anything that's going on!"

Lifting her chin, Kathleen looked him square in the face and tried to control the trembling in her voice.

"That night you came to get me. Remember? That's when it started."

He narrowed his eyes at her. "You mean that stuff with the books?"

"Yes. And everyone tried to tell me things were just coincidences, that everything could be explained, but now—now look what's happened!" She looked pleadingly at him, through a sudden mist of tears. "Don't you see?" she whispered. "I think I'm going to be next!"

For a long moment he was silent. Kathleen grabbed his arm and peered hard into his face.

"First it was you and Della . . . then Monica . . . then Vivian . . . now Robin. Tonight someone locked me in the library—I think they're going to try to kill me next—only I don't know *why!* I don't know why any of this is happening!"

Bran ran a hand slowly back through his hair. "Jesus," he whispered. "We gotta get out of here. We gotta get some help."

Kathleen hurried over to the desk and picked up the phone. She dialed 911, listened for a minute, then slammed the receiver down again.

"The lines must be out," she said tightly. "There's no dial tone."

"There has to be. The storm's not that bad yet."

"Listen for yourself."

But instead he grabbed her arm. "Come on, let's go out the back."

Kathleen was shaking so hard, she could hardly walk. *Robin . . . Robin . . .* She could still see his eyes staring at her—those beautiful, empty eyes—how long had he laid there struggling for life while she went about her normal business of the day? Why Robin? Who could have done such a thing?

"A person with no conscience . . ."

In that instant she could hear Alexander's voice again, far, far back in her mind, and her blood went icy cold.

"Kath!" Bran hissed at her. "Hurry!"

He pushed her, and she ran. She could hear him behind her as they sped through the dark rooms, and as she came into the kitchen, she grabbed her coat and purse and raced to the door.

"There's a phone at the drugstore, Bran—it's only a few blocks away. Do you think you can make it, or do you want to wait for me outside?"

He didn't answer, and as Kathleen pulled on the door, she repeated the question.

"Bran, do you want to wait here while I get help? Or do you think you can walk?"

Still no reply. Now, with patience snapping, she whirled around. "Bran, did you hear—"

Kathleen's eyes went wide, sweeping the kitchen at a glance.

The room was empty.

Bran wasn't there.

"Bran?" she said tremulously. "Bran, where are you?"

No answer.

Stunned, Kathleen moved slowly across the floor, her eyes trying to probe every dark crevice and corner. This wasn't the time for tricks or jokes . . . she couldn't believe Bran would be so insensitive . . . this wasn't like him . . . but what else could it be . . . ?

"Bran, I mean it, stop fooling around!"

Her voice shook dangerously. She crept through the doorway and into the adjoining room. Bookshelves were everywhere . . . bookshelves and shadows. Kathleen swallowed hard and crept forward.

"Bran . . . Bran, please answer me. . . ."

Her mouth felt like cotton. She could hardly breathe. She was painfully cold, and fear prickled over every inch of her body.

"Oh, God, Bran, please *answer* me!"

Silence rushed through her head, and Kathleen felt dizzy from the force of it. *He was right behind me. . . . I heard him right behind me. . . . Maybe he fell . . . maybe his leg gave out and he fell. . . .*

That was it. Of course, that *had* to be it.

She passed the first aisle of bookshelves and

nervously glanced down the length of it. She passed the second . . . the third. Something whispered along the floor . . . slithered through the shadows —and instantly she froze. The wind?

Footsteps?

An image flashed back to her without warning— only a few nights ago the sound she'd heard in the library—as though someone had pulled back into the corner, trying to hide.

"Bran?" she whispered. "Is that you?"

She could hear her heart beating in the awful stillness.

Then . . . the sound came again.

And it *was* a footstep—she was sure of it now—a slow and cautious tread upon a creaking floorboard . . . as someone moved stealthily, not wanting to be heard. . . .

Kathleen froze.

She opened her mouth to call his name . . . but her words stuck fast in her throat.

Bran . . . oh, God, Bran . . . where are you!

She forced herself to go on.

Forced herself to go past the rows and rows of bookshelves, and then suddenly she turned down one narrow aisle and slipped swiftly through the shadows. She stopped again . . . listened.

The quiet went on forever.

She closed her eyes—tried to muffle the raspy sound of her breathing.

She heard a faint footfall. The soft, light stirring of air . . .

In that instant Kathleen knew that whoever it was stood right on the other side of the bookcase. That if she reached up and pulled one book from its place on the shelf, she'd be face to face with the intruder.

The murderer.

Had he killed Bran? Was Bran lying somewhere even now, like Robin was lying all alone in the back room? A scream of pain, of rage, echoed through her head, yet made no sound. She stood there, rooted to the spot with terror, and she could hear him breathing—could actually hear him *breathing* —softly, calmly, as the footsteps began to move away once more.

She waited till they reached the opposite end of the aisle.

And then she bolted.

She ran to the kitchen and flung herself at the back door, and she wrestled frantically with the lock.

She couldn't hear the footsteps anymore.

There was only the dark, dead silence.

Without warning the door burst open, throwing Kathleen back against the counter. In that split second she recognized Alexander standing there, blocking her way.

"Kathleen," he murmured, "where's the fire?"

"Oh, God . . . no . . ."

She waited till he was almost across the threshold. And then she sprang forward, shoving the door into him as hard as she could. The impact knocked him backward, and she squeezed frantically through the door and tried to jump over him as he sprawled in the doorway.

His hand shot out and caught her ankle.

Screaming, she angled her foot down and stomped.

She heard his cry of pain. She felt his fingers slide away, and she jerked free, toppling backward onto a pile of old lumber. Without thinking, she grabbed up a board, and as Alexander stumbled to his feet, she hit him as hard as she could. She saw his body crumple to the floor—his arm flinging out in one last effort to catch her—and she scrambled sideways out of his reach.

She hadn't noticed how close she was to the edge of the porch.

Now as her foot slipped off, she felt herself falling, and she flung out her arms to catch herself. Flailing wildly, she tried to find something—anything—to hold on to. There was a thud as her head made contact with the steps.

Rain and wind roared through her mind . . .

And out of the darkness a face slowly began to materialize.

It was a familiar face.

Gazing down at her with a strange, strange smile.

"Thank God," Kathleen gasped. "Thank God you're back—"

"Yes," Miss Finch said, even as she faded . . . drifting into blackness. "And I got here just in time."

Bran?" Kathleen mumbled.

Everything was fuzzy . . . blurred. She had the vague sensation of cold and damp and deep, dead silence.

"Bran . . ." she mumbled again. "Where are you?"

"Don't worry, Kathleen," said a voice. "You'll be with him soon enough."

And *I know that voice*, Kathleen thought groggily, *I know that voice . . . knew that voice . . . someone . . . someone close . . .*

The fear came then without warning. It washed over her in icy waves and squeezed around her heart.

"Bran," she pleaded.

Her eyelids struggled open. Pain shot through her head, and she remembered the porch, remembered falling. Squinting her eyes, she strained to see through the gloom. One small cone of light shone from a lamp in the corner, and as she tried to focus on it, barred windows and peeling walls slowly materialized around her. She was in the children's room. She could hear rain beating on the roof. And someone was beside her, sitting there with her on the floor, propped heavily against her shoulder as though he were asleep.

"Bran?" she whispered.

With an effort she lifted her hand and groped out. Her fingers brushed the fabric of a sleeve and trailed slowly down the length of a cold, cold arm.

Kathleen gasped and jerked away. For one second she got a glimpse of Robin's bloody face before he keeled slowly sideways and slumped across her lap. Screaming, she shoved him away and stumbled to her feet, then froze in terror as a shadow stirred softly beside the window.

"Keep your voice down, Kathleen," Miss Finch murmured. "You're in the library, after all."

She was staring out at the storm, her back stiff and straight.

She hardly even seemed to be breathing.

Kathleen threw a wild glance at the body on the floor. The sick taste of fear rose in her throat, and as she choked it back down, she began edging along the wall toward the doorway.

"I'm going for help, Miss Finch." Her mind was racing, even as she fought to keep her voice calm. "I'm going to call an ambulance."

"No, Kathleen. You're not going to call anyone."

Miss Finch turned slightly, looking back over her

shoulder. As lightning stabbed beyond the window-pane, Kathleen saw the woman's eyes caught in a split-second glow.

She saw their fixed stare . . .

Their frightening emptiness.

"I have to kill you," Miss Finch said quietly. "Now you've seen me. Now you could tell people. So I really don't have any alternative."

"Miss Finch . . . please . . ." Kathleen's voice broke. She pressed her spine hard against the wall and drew a deep, ragged breath. "Why are you doing this? Let me get someone to help you—"

"Sit down, Kathleen."

Kathleen looked desperately at the door. Where was Bran? What had happened to Alexander?

"I said, sit *down*, Kathleen!" Miss Finch repeated sharply. She turned around then. She seemed to be holding something, and as her arm lifted into the air, Kathleen could see the gun clutched in her hand.

Very slowly Kathleen lowered herself to the floor. After several seconds Miss Finch nodded and began to speak.

"Once upon a time, there was a girl who fell in love with a handsome young man. She would have done anything for him . . . given him anything. But he married someone else."

Miss Finch hesitated . . . gazed up at the ceiling. In her hand the gun trembled slightly.

"He married someone else," she mumbled. "And they had a daughter."

Again she stopped. A quick stab of pain went

across her face, and slowly she turned her eyes from the ceiling onto Kathleen.

"You could have been mine, Kathleen. You *should* have been mine."

"Miss Finch," Kathleen whispered, "what are you talking about?"

"It's a popular rumor, you know," the woman went on, and she was nodding now, nodding her head up and down, up and down, as the words tumbled out. "You know the one, Kathleen. That I was in love once. The love of a lifetime, the love of my life. That he left me. That . . ."

She caught herself. Her body stiffened, and the gun aimed directly at Kathleen's head.

"I *loved* your father, Kathleen. More than anything in the world. Only . . . he loved your mother more."

And Kathleen could hear her father's voice again, all those discussions about Miss Finch, all the times she'd made fun of the librarian like everyone else in town had done all these long years—*"Miss Finch is younger than she looks, Kathleen. . . . You shouldn't judge her too harshly. . . . You never know what happens in people's lives to make them turn out the way they do. . . ."*

"I could have left," Miss Finch said softly, and Kathleen snapped back to attention. "I could have, but I chose not to. I stayed right here in Fremont. So I could watch him being happy. So I could watch him have the home and family I always wanted."

She paused again . . . gave a short laugh.

"And then your mother left. And it was a miracle, really—I *knew* it was a miracle—the one I'd prayed for all these years! I knew I'd been given a second chance."

Kathleen was shaking all over. She felt tears brim in her eyes, and she forcibly blinked them away.

"Only one problem now," Miss Finch said thoughtfully. "You."

The gun was no longer quivering. Miss Finch was gripping it with both hands, and she took a step forward as she talked.

"You're not so different, Kathleen—you laugh behind my back just like the others. Don't you think I know how people make *fun* of me? How they've been trying to get rid of me for *years?* So I thought about this for a very long time. Very, very carefully."

Her mouth moved in a wistful smile. She made a gesture with the gun.

"And I decided to get rid of the other young people around you. A rash of teenage killings? People would think it's some serial killer who hates kids and your father would send you to live with your mother."

Kathleen shut her eyes. A wave of nausea washed over her and she swallowed hard, then forced herself to meet Miss Finch's eyes.

"Where's Bran?" she asked. "What did you do with him?"

She watched as Miss Finch backed toward the window. The woman shook her head, her shoulders heaving in a sigh.

"Why should you have someone you care about, Kathleen?" she said tonelessly. "I couldn't."

"What did you do to him!"

"No one will ever suspect me. I'm the mean town librarian, away at a seminar. I'm just plain old Miss Finch, someone to laugh at, someone to get rid of." Her mouth twisted into a tight smile. "Bran and Della . . . Robin and Alexander . . . Monica and Vivian—"

"Vivian," Kathleen choked. "Where's Viv?"

"They'll find her eventually, come high tide. Well . . . she did want to go to the beach, didn't she?"

Miss Finch reached off into the shadows. A moment later she walked over to Kathleen, the gun held steady, her other hand holding a cup.

"I'm only doing this for your father, Kathleen. Only for him. My one concession, so you won't have to suffer." She thrust the cup nearer. "Drink it."

Kathleen stared at the cup, at the liquid spilling a little over the tilted rim. She shook her head and leaned tighter against the wall.

"Go on, it's all right," Miss Finch coaxed her. "They're yours, after all. The pills Dr. McNally gave you. You won't feel a thing."

This time Kathleen couldn't hold back the tears. They filled her eyes and trailed slowly down her cheeks. She heard the hammer click on the gun. . . . She lifted her hand and took the cup from Miss Finch.

"That's it, Kathleen, go on and drink it. Believe me, it's much better this way."

Kathleen stared at the cup. She gripped it hard, unable to move.

"If you *don't* drink it," Miss Finch mumbled, "then you'll *never* find out where Bran is."

Kathleen gave a silent sob. Very slowly she put the cup to her lips. She took a small swallow.

"All of it," Miss Finch whispered.

A sudden defiance surged through her. Kathleen gulped in a huge mouthful of liquid, working her cheeks and throat muscles, making choking sounds, while trying frantically not to swallow.

Smiling, Miss Finch turned back to the window. Kathleen let the liquid dribble from the sides of her mouth and rested her head back against the wall. It'd been impossible to store it all—she knew she'd swallowed some of it. But how much? How much would it take to knock her out?

"When I get home from my seminar, you'll be gone," Miss Finch said matter-of-factly. "They'll find you and Robin in here where both of you were working so diligently. Your poor father will be quite heartbroken. Without you and your mother, he'll only have me."

She turned and stared at Kathleen. Kathleen let her eyes droop shut, her head loll to her shoulder. She *was* a little drowsy, she could *feel* it, spreading through her, slow and warm . . . *Oh, no, God, please*—

"Only me," Miss Finch murmured.

Kathleen's eyelids fluttered open. She saw the gun aimed at her head. She saw Miss Finch's hand tightening on the trigger. . . .

Kathleen felt herself slouch sideways, felt her body go limp.

She heard Miss Finch walk across the floor and stop beside her.

"Bran," Kathleen mumbled. "Where is he? You said you'd tell me. . . ."

She struggled to look up, struggled to focus.

She saw Miss Finch above her . . . saw the gun pull slowly out of sight.

"Find the clue, Kathleen." Miss Finch smiled. And then she was gone.

23

Footsteps hurried down the corridor, fading to silence.

With a sob Kathleen pushed herself away from the wall and stumbled to her feet.

Her head throbbed—all fire and pain. Holding on to the wall, she staggered across the room and peeked cautiously out into the hall.

Her mind whirled with thoughts of death—of murder—and the throbbing grew more furious. She had no idea what Miss Finch had meant— where Miss Finch had gone—if she'd try and come back. She couldn't even think what might have happened to Bran and Alexander.

She had to find them.

She had to hurry.

Kathleen turned around, eyes squeezing shut. Furiously she fought back tears, trying to clear her head, calm herself down. She opened her eyes once more, and her gaze fell instantly on Robin, sprawled across the floor.

He was lying on something.

She could see it, just a small section of binding and crumpled pages, sticking out from underneath his legs.

He must have been holding it. . . .

It must have been in his lap when I pushed him over. . . .

Slowly Kathleen walked over to Robin. Taking hold of the book, she began to pull, heart hammering furiously as she tried not to touch the dead body. With one final tug the book came free, and she held it to the light to read the title.

HOW GREEN WAS MY VALLEY.

Kathleen stared at it, frowning.

Something . . . something . . . but what?

She swayed a little on her feet. Taking a deep breath, she went to the door again and looked out. Her mind didn't seem to be functioning very fast; her thoughts were all dazed and confused. She held on to the doorframe and angrily willed the pain from her head.

Something in that book . . . the clue . . . what is it?

She bit her lip and tried to concentrate.

The life of a family—yes, that's it—a family in Wales . . . coal miners . . . and there's an explosion . . . the mine caves in . . .

"Oh, God," she whispered. "Oh, no . . ."

A rush of strength went through her then. Strength and dread and terror—all of them at once—propelling her down the hallway. She kept close to the wall, trying not to make a sound. If Miss Finch heard her, she'd have no more chances.

None at all.

Please . . . please . . . I've got to make it. . . .

The door to the main room was standing open.

As Kathleen hurried past the desk, past rows and rows of books, she felt curiously dreamlike. Everything looked old and familiar, shabby and tired. Everything just as it should be. . . .

Yet something was wrong.

She could feel it in every sense of her being— could almost seem to smell it, even—it was there in her mind and in her eyes and the back of her throat, even the pores of her skin—every nerve was on edge, alerting her, *something wrong, so very, very wrong—*

She made her way through the dark, empty chambers, slipping noiselessly like a shadow, terror mounting with every step. She reached the kitchen at last, and she shoved on the door, bursting breathlessly out into the room.

Immediately she choked and fell back. The room reeked of gas, and as Kathleen felt a hot swell of bile rise up into her throat, she glanced over at the kitchen stove. She could see the oven door hanging open . . . could hear the burners hissing . . . and she hurried over to turn them off. Staring down in disbelief, it took her a minute to realize that all the knobs were missing.

"Oh, no—"

Kathleen whirled around. As a flash of lightning ripped the sky, she could see Miss Finch running across the yard, away from the building in the direction of the street.

"Bran!" Kathleen screamed. "Alexander!"

She had no idea where they were—if they were even still alive. As in a nightmare, she ran back again, searching through all the rooms on both floors. Then suddenly a memory broke through her panic.

Coal mines . . . underground . . .

The basement.

And *of course,* she thought from some remaining scrap of sanity, *of course, like the mines, so when the building blows up, they'll both be buried, dead or alive. . . .*

She raced back to the kitchen. She flung open the basement door and went down.

She was gagging now, fighting to breathe. The cloying sweetness of gas filled her head and her throat, and she clung to the stairway banister, dizzy and light-headed. The dank coolness of the basement rushed up to meet her, and she drank it in greedily, taking deep gulps of it into her lungs.

"Bran! Where are you!"

She froze, thinking she'd heard a noise.

A muffled cry? It was hard to be sure.

Instinctively she followed it, feeling her way along the slimy walls. Scarcely any light came in through the tiny windows—only the faintest glow of lampposts on the streets outside. She searched for a lightswitch, then realized in a sudden panic that it could mean instant death.

"Bran!" she screamed. "Answer me!"

Again she thought she heard something. She started toward it, then stumbled and fell, striking her head on the wall, scraping her arms on nail-studded boards. She managed to get back up again and kept on. She rounded a corner into another, deeper part of the cellar, and then suddenly she stopped, gazing in horror at what she saw.

Bran was on the floor, his mouth gagged, his hands bound behind him and fixed to a pipe on the wall. Across from him Alexander was lying in a slimy pool of water, his hands also bound to the basement wall. As Kathleen got a glimpse of him, she felt sick. His glasses were gone; his hair was clotted with blood. He looked like he'd been dragged over the floor, facedown.

"Bran," Kathleen choked. "Oh, Bran . . ."

Quickly she pulled the rag from his mouth. With a sigh of relief Bran tried to scoot himself around so she could reach the ropes on his hands.

"It's Miss Finch, Kath," he burst out. His eyes were wide with shock and disbelief. "She jumped me from behind when I was following you. I never even saw her—she came out between the shelves and hit me over the head with something. I must have passed out and—" He broke off, sniffing the air. "What's that? It smells like gas."

Her hands were shaking so bad, she couldn't untie him. Fumbling with the knots, she sat back on her heels and gave a cry of despair.

"I can't get them off—they're too tight!"

"There must be something around here you can use!" Bran's eyes made a quick search of the room. "Go help Alexander."

Kathleen nodded and crawled over to him. As she pulled off his gag, Alexander coughed a few times and took a deep breath.

"It *is* gas." He coughed again. "What's happening?"

"She put it on upstairs," Kathleen babbled. "She took the knobs off the stove—I can't turn it off!"

Alexander gave a wry smile. "Not that it would take much to blow this place apart. Get out of here, Kathleen."

"He's right, Kath—you've got to go," Bran insisted. His voice was low and urgent. "Do you hear me?"

"No. I won't leave you!"

"You've got to. Listen to me, Kath—I *want* you to!"

"No!" She caught Bran's face between her hands and forced a smile through her tears. "Dying won't do you any good, Bran Vanelli, you're still going to be stuck with me."

"We're all going to be stuck to every available surface if we don't get out of here," Alexander reminded them calmly. "Break the window, Kathleen. Use the glass."

Nodding, she scrambled over to the open window. She pulled the sleeve of her sweater down over her good hand, then swung it hard against the glass. As it shattered onto the floor, Kathleen picked up the sharpest piece and began sawing furiously at Bran's ropes.

"This makes me a little nervous"—Alexander sighed—"that she brought *you* the glass and not me."

Bran gave a weak grin. "If I get out, I'll carry you."

"That's a relief."

Kathleen kept working. Even with the window open, the gas was getting worse in here. Her lungs felt as if they were closing up on her; both Bran and

Alexander were coughing. At last Kathleen felt the rope give, and Bran immediately yanked his hands apart. He grabbed the glass away from her and attacked Alexander's bonds with a vengeance.

"Hurry," Kathleen begged. "Hurry—"

She watched in a sort of daze as Bran kept raking the glass back and forth across the ropes. She heard the sharp intake of Alexander's breath as Bran accidentally sliced into his hand—she saw the blood on Bran's fingers where he'd cut himself. Without warning the ropes flew free, and Bran pulled Alexander to his feet. Then both of them grabbed Kathleen and pushed her toward the broken window.

"No!" she yelled. "I won't go first! I'm not going without you!"

"Get her up there," Bran ordered. He shoved her into Alexander's arms, and she felt herself being shoved out through the small opening.

Kathleen tumbled out onto the grass. Catching her breath, she crawled back to the window and reached in to help. It was Bran who came out next, Alexander who insisted on bringing up the rear. As Alexander hit the ground, the three of them took off running.

The explosion catapulted them through the yard.

As Kathleen lay there, stunned, she felt the sky falling down around her. Instinctively she put her arms over her head and lay still, waiting for the earth to stop shaking beneath her.

"Bran," she murmured, "Alexander—"

She couldn't seem to get up. She was flattened

into the mud, and she was suddenly too exhausted to move.

Got to find Bran . . . Alexander . . .

She forced her head up. To her surprise, people were running toward her across the yard, a whole crowd of them,—police and firefighters and people she recognized—

"Dad!" she cried. "Mrs. Vanelli!"

"My God, Kathleen, are you all right?" With one strong swoop, her father grabbed her up and hugged her. "Kathleen . . . here she is, Rosa! Are you all *right?"* he asked again, only this time he pulled back to take a long look at her.

"Dad, what are you doing here? Where's Bran?"

Mrs. Vanelli was hugging her now, crying, asking where Bran was. Kathleen thought she heard him calling her name, but she couldn't find him through the smoke. It was total confusion—firefighters yelling and hauling equipment, people screaming, police struggling to control the growing mob. Kathleen tried to twist free, but her father was holding her again, and she couldn't get loose. "Dad, you've got to find Bran and Alexander—"

"I went straight to Rosa's the minute I got back in town," her father was saying. "We were standing right there at her front door when we heard an explosion—"

"I'm okay, Dad, I'm okay. Please—you've got to find—"

"Look!" someone shouted. "It's Miss Finch!"

As everyone turned, they saw the librarian standing on the front walkway, a small dark figure silhouetted against the roaring flames.

"Miss Finch!" a fireman yelled. "Miss Finch, get back!"

"What's she doing?" Mrs. Vanelli cried. "Is she crazy?"

Yet even from here, Kathleen *knew* what Miss Finch was doing, could *feel* her fury and her despair as she stood alone, gazing at Kathleen and her father.

"Wait here!" Mr. Davies ordered, and before Kathleen could stop him, he began running toward the library.

"Dad!" Kathleen screamed.

"Madeline!" he cried. "Get away from the building!"

Kathleen saw the firefighter sprinting across the yard . . . saw him tackling her father even as Mr. Davies fought desperately to get to Miss Finch.

"Look! The whole roof's going!"

"Everyone get back!"

Kathleen saw her father being forced away.

She heard him shouting—*pleading*—at Miss Finch to save herself.

For a moment Kathleen almost thought she would.

But then, as everyone watched in horror, Miss Finch turned and walked calmly through the front door, into the library.

h, no," Bran groaned. "It's *alive!*"

From her hospital bed Della glared at him, then waved at Kathleen, who stood behind him in the doorway.

"Why did they let you in?" she asked Bran. "There's a special ward for people like you."

Beside her, Mrs. Vanelli got up from a chair and shook a finger at Bran. "You! You should thank God every day for a friend like Della!"

"Yeah, I'd thank Him if she was somebody *else's* friend," Bran grumbled. He winced as his mother whacked him on the shoulder with her purse.

"Look at him," she fussed, going to Della, straightening the sheets, *"this* is my contribution to the world."

"I'm really sorry," Della said sympathetically.

"Hey"—Bran frowned—"is that any way to talk to me? After I went and spent money on you?"

"You bought a one-way plane ticket? To another dimension?"

"You *are* another dimension. Look, it's candy." He sauntered over and dropped the box onto the covers. Cautiously Della lifted the lid and peeked inside while Kathleen perched on the end of the bed.

"They're okay, Del, I already checked them out for you," she promised, indicating the one empty spot in the middle.

"This is too much. All he does is insult my size, then he brings me chocolates, for God's sake." Della sighed. "If anything good has come out of this whole ordeal, I've actually lost weight."

Bran grinned and kissed the top of her head. "I think you're beautiful."

"That's it. Call the orderlies. He's totally over the edge."

"Del, look. I brought a friend," Kathleen said, smiling and motioning Alexander to come in.

Della squinted and looked him up and down. "Ummm . . . very nice."

Alexander stared back, unabashed. "Alexander Hodges. The third."

"Della Conway. The knockout," she retorted. "Nice to meet you, Al." She winked and turned her attention back to Kathleen. "So how're things at home these days?"

"Good. No, I mean, really good. Dad's spending lots of time with me. *Too* much time—he's starting to drive me crazy."

"He almost lost you. That does something to parents."

"Does it? Bran's mom tries to lose him all the time."

"Good point."

Bran ignored them and started digging through the box. "Any of that cherry stuff in here?"

"Ycch!" Della shuddered. "You *would* like those, of course. You're so disgusting."

Bran looked her squarely in the face and popped a whole candy into his mouth, never changing expressions.

"So, Al, what happened to your face?" Della asked.

"Alexander," he said evenly. "Kathleen stepped on it."

Kathleen cringed. "Well, I didn't mean to. It's just that when I thought he was after me, I tried to knock him out."

"Could this be the reason she never has dates?" Bran deadpanned.

"Speaking of dates, do you have a girlfriend?" Della asked Alexander.

He glanced from Kathleen to Bran. "Apparently not."

"You want one? I'm available."

Bran started choking, and Kathleen hit him on the back. "Go get some water or something. We don't want you dying here in Della's room."

"Yes, we do," Della insisted. "But I only want to watch if he's in deep and unbearable agony."

"I've *been* in deep and unbearable agony ever since I had to look at you."

"Will you two stop it?" Kathleen laughed. She followed Bran out to the water fountain and leaned against the wall, giving him a sidelong glance.

"I'm glad she's going to be okay. Once she finally gets out of here . . . has some therapy . . . she'll be good as new."

"That certainly makes my day."

"You're terrible. You wouldn't know what to do if you didn't have Della to fight with."

She could tell he was hiding a smile. "Right. I'd just be so lost."

Kathleen punched him on the shoulder, then took a deep breath, her smile fading. "Poor Miss Finch. I can't stop thinking about her."

"I know. Me, too. It's hard to believe."

"I don't think the police *would* have believed me if they hadn't found all that stuff in her house." Kathleen sighed. "She had everything written down, all planned out and organized and filed away."

"Except the stuff about your dad."

She nodded unhappily. "Except for that."

Bran was quiet for a long moment. "You're never gonna tell that part, are you."

"No. It'd be too painful for everyone. And right now things are . . . you know . . . so much better. Mom and I are even talking again. And I'm actually going to visit her and see her new place."

"I'm glad, Kath." Bran smiled. "Your dad's finally acting like a dad. And your mom's finally getting her head together. And *you're* finally getting a little happiness in your life. Yeah, I'd say you're overdue."

"Actually, I'd say I'm still mixed up about a lot of things."

"Try *most* things."

"Okay, most things. Except for . . . well . . . maybe *one* thing."

Bran wiped his mouth with the back of his hand. "Yeah, I know. You love me."

Flushing, Kathleen scowled at him, but he only shook his head and gave a long-suffering sigh.

"Yeah, you do, Kath. Always have. More now than ever. I *told* you, you can't fool me."

"Oh, Bran, in your dreams."

"Come on, I even turned down a trip to the beach with Monica Franklin, 'cause I knew you couldn't live without me over spring break."

Kathleen stared at him. "She asked you to go to the beach with her?"

"Sure. But I said no, and she told me just what she thought of me. Which wasn't a whole hell of a lot."

"So that's what the note meant," Kathleen murmured.

"What note?"

"Nothing," she said quickly. To her surprise Bran leaned forward, resting his palms flat against the wall on either side of her head. Then he tilted his face so he could stare into her eyes.

"Look, this is the way I figure it. You hardly date at all. And when you do, they're stupid." As she opened her mouth to protest, he put his hand over it and shook his head. "And me—I date all these girls. But somehow I just never commit . . . you know? Now, why *is* that, you think?"

Kathleen said nothing. Bran's voice lowered even more.

"They're not you," he said quietly.

He took his hand away from her mouth . . . put his lips there instead. His kiss was deep and slow.

"Growing up . . . going out . . . college . . . that's nothing, Kath. This time I almost lost you for good." He touched her cheek with his fingertips and smiled. "No more, okay?"

Kathleen nodded, dazed. "Okay," she breathed. She felt light-headed and warm all over. As Bran pulled away and reached for her hand, she walked with him back to Della's room. Alexander was standing beside the bed, arms crossed over his chest, absorbed in conversation. Mrs. Vanelli tiptoed over to join them in the doorway.

"Listen," she whispered, nodding toward the bed, clasping her hands together. "Love talk. I can hear it a mile away."

"Ma, it's not a mile. It's more like three feet."

"Well, you listen to me, Mr. Hormones—if you knew what was good for you, you'd start thinking seriously about—"

"Kathleen?" he asked, and she broke off in surprise. "Yeah, well, I'm gonna start thinking about her. Just to shut all of you up."

His mother beamed. She reached over and pinched his cheek while Bran tried to squirm out of her grasp.

"Forget it." Mrs. Vanelli smiled. "She's much too good for you."

"It's okay," Kathleen said, straightfaced, "I've decided to lower my standards *considerably.*"

And as Bran rubbed at the red mark on his cheek, she reached up and gave him a kiss.